BATTLESUIT BASTARDS

CASTALIA HOUSE

QUANTUM MORTIS

WARDOGS

BATTLESUIT BASTARDS

G.D. STARK

CASTALIA HOUSE

Battlesuit Bastards

G.D. Stark

Published by Castalia House
Tampere, Finland
www.castaliahouse.com

Cover: Steve Beaulieu
Editor: Vox Day
Created by Vox Day

ISBN: 978-952-7065-08-2

Contents

Chapter 1

Easy Money

KA-CHING!

That's what I heard. You might have heard the sound of an I-128 ceramic frag grenade going off, followed by two newly dead bodies falling to the deck, but the violence sounded like money to me.

"Dammit, Tommy—you're on top again!" Park's voice crackled through my earpiece. He'd seen the kill stats increment in my favor.

I didn't have the chance to reply, as a bolt of fire shot past me— too close. My suit armor could probably handle it, but I wasn't about to take any stupid chances. Instead, I hit the deck and rolled behind a support column. It wasn't much, but it was better than nothing. But the cargo bay was supposed to be empty. I keyed my transceiver. "Sergeant, we have contact in cargo."

"Hang on, Falkland. We're on the way," Sergeant Hanley replied. Then Ace's voice came back from our ship, low and clear. "We have nothing living on scan, Falkland. Probably shielded. Use caution."

"Roger, sir," I said. "Falkland out–"

A laser bolt burned into the deck six inches from my face, cutting me off. My visor darkened for a second to compensate, then a second bolt hit me in the back. Damage was minimal but my lower back was a mess of electric tingling. That shot—from above?

I looked up and saw a hostile perched on the girders, crouched above the bay like a monkey with a beamer and quickly snapped off a pair of shots. One missed, but he took the other full in the chest, knocking him off his perch and down to the deck with a nasty crunch. No armor on that one, just like the rest. Our armor gave us an unfair advantage over the near-helpless crew; even when they hit us, they couldn't hurt us.

Another bolt blazed past me, this time from my level. "Sergeant, you guys planning on showing up anytime soon?" I hissed into my transceiver. He and Park were clearing the crew quarters while I was supposed to lock down this supposedly empty cargo bay. We didn't usually split up while clearing a ship, but this was just a civilian freighter that wasn't prepared for pirates, let alone professional mercs.

"Sergeant?" I said again. "They've got at least two more here, could use some backup." No reply for a minute, then I heard Jock. "Sit tight, Tommy. We're coming."

Sitting tight was easier said than done. I was too exposed and there were no telling how many more crewmen were in the bay. Barrels, crates, forklifts—it was a confusing mess of potential hiding spots. The three I'd already killed since busting in obviously had more friends. They must have decided to take refuge here in the hopes of ambushing our boarding party.

I saw a head pop up behind a water tote and winged off a bolt. Miss. Then two more bolts flew past me from the left. I turned to shoot—then *CRACK*—something blew my elbow off from the right. Not my actual elbow, of course, but my exo's. It felt like fire. Foam filled the crack and a jolt of some fancy painkiller numbed the area. Space! That wasn't an energy weapon—that was a projectile! No time to think on it—back it up, Tommy—back through the door—now! I scrabbled backward, ducking low—then a plasma bolt nailed me in the chest, knocking me on my tail. I was still outnumbered 3–1 even after wasting the first three marks. *Dammit, where are Jock and Park?*

I crawled rapidly back towards the open door, red warning light glowing around me from the breached seal indicator from when I'd force-popped the door with my wrist chip. I jumped up and ran through as more plasma spattered against the walls.

The main lights were out and the corridor was filled with smoke. My optics compensated just in time for me to see another team member. Onboard ID told me it was Jock. The other guy behind him didn't register. Park, offline. The other five in the boarding party must still be on the bridge. I backed away from the door and kept it covered as we met up.

"Status, Tommy?" Jock said.

"Bay has multiple hostiles, sergeant. Three down. I'd guess at least three left."

Jock frowned. "Surprise, surprise. Intel had it wrong again."

"Not the first time," I grimaced, looking at the mess of foam surrounding my elbow. My wounded arm was locked in place now. Fortunately, it was my right.

Jock whistled. "What did that?"

"Not plasma," I said. "Projectile." Projectile weapons were not standard space issue because they tended to punch holes through things, yet some idiot in the crew had been carrying one anyhow.

"Red Team has the bridge locked down. Want to call them in or spin the wheel for cash and prizes?"

I looked back at the cargo bay door, now silent. The surviving crew members were in there. Probably edging up towards the corridor right now, scared as hell, but determined to take us with them.

"If we had a few ceramics left I'd feel more enthusiastic," I said.

I could see Jock's grin through his visor as he pulled a pair of I-128s from the back of his belt.

"Two enough?"

"Yeah, let's go for it," I said, locking one onto my Cerberus M-92 carbine as Jock mounted the second on his. "What's up with your bucket, Park?"

Park shrugged as he put his helmet back on. "Chips are shot, armor is sound," he declared. That meant his targeting and infostream was dead. Not what you want from the team sniper.

"Got a plan?" Jock said.

I thought back on the configuration of the cargo bay. The entrance was about twelve meters long, check-in window and office door on the right at about four meters, then you reached wide-open bay except for the chunky support columns. Great big interior, flat metal plate floor, lots of crates towards the back, lots of open space in the middle. A direct assault was out. Our frags would take them out easily, given their lack of armor, but first we had to figure out where they were.

So, we had to make them show their cards. Jock had the same thought. He thumped Park on the shoulder and tapped his helmet to his. "Hey cowboy, you got no targeting, so you'll have to draw their fire."

Park shrugged and clicked the lock on his bucket. Usually he was the squad's preferred shooter, but even the best sniper couldn't spot and shoot faster blind than an enhanced shooter. Once they honed in on him, our comps could give us locations. And it wouldn't be too dangerous. He had his armor, we'd be right behind him, and these guys were just crew, or at most, glorified security guards. No sweat.

"Just watch out for the projectile guy," Jock said to Park, as if that were possible.

We edged up to the door and I looked inside the bay. View was clear.

"Alright, it's Leroy time," Jock told Park.

Park nodded, set his Cerberus on full auto, wide dispersal, then sprinted like a madman into the bay, his battlesuit juicing his steps and turning him into a death-dealing grasshopper. A split second later, we followed him. Park was well in front of us, bounding quickly across the bay. Jock and I split up and took up positions by the wall on either side of the entrance. Plasma zipped towards Park from the left—and then a projectile weapon shot from the right. 10 o'clock, 3 o'clock. Jock and I fired almost simultaneously, as our auto-aiming AIs triangulated the incoming fire sources for us.

Thump CRACK! Jock's grenade exploded less than 10 meters from me. I heard the tinkle of ceramic shrapnel shattering against my armor.

The grenade had torn apart a crewman to my left; he seemed to be still breathing so I put a bolt through his head to put him out of his misery. The job is the job, but I don't like to see people in unnecessary pain.

Park had rolled to the deck by a stack of barrels just before the explosions. Now he stood, back to the cargo, looking side to side for any remaining danger.

The bay was silent. If there were any targets left, they had the good sense to quit firing.

Jock and I cased the edges of the room, backs to the walls. Shelving towered overhead in front of me. My heart thumped; I was still amped. I cross the bay to see where my grenade had popped. Yep, the guy was most definitely dead. The ceramic frag grenades were designed for in-ship use; they made short work of flesh without penetrating metal. No use killing the bad guys then getting sucked out into space. On the ground next to the crewman lay a civilian-grade plasma carbine of cheap Gorwagese manufacture. "Two more down in here, Sergeant Hanley," I said. "You find the slug-thrower yet?"

"Slug-thrower?" came a thick smoker's voice, "What dumbass had a slug-thrower?" It was Squid. He'd been a captain in the Navy. But in the company, he was only a master sergeant. By all rights, he should have been staff officer, but he'd gotten sick of paperwork and decided to get back into the action when he went private sector.

"Clearing cargo bay, Sarge," Jock said. "We hit some minor resistance here. Nothing we can't handle, over."

"Roger," Squid replied.

A minute later I reached the back of the cargo bay, meeting Park. The computer gave me nothing to target, so we waited. A minute later, Jock arrived, holding up an ancient slug-thrower.

"Stupid kid," he growled. "Had a hunting rifle. Something called a Maywin. Maybe T7 at most."

I glanced at the stats board. 13 kills were now registered.

"I got two," Jock said, answering before I said anything. "The other one wasn't armed. Just a techie."

He spoke into his transceiver. "Sergeant, we're all clear here. Just engineering left."

"Roger," Squid answered. "The bridge is secure. We've got her about tied up here, then we'll come down and clear engineering with you."

We took up defensive positions in the room, just in case, and maintained them until he arrived. I was pissed about my elbow. This contract should have been a cakewalk. Damn pop gun!

Every contract was different. Sometimes we got to loot, sometimes we didn't. Sometimes we got bonuses for knocking out vehicles or beacons or whatnot, sometimes we were just playing babysitters for scared corporates or politicos with more cash than security knowhow. Those were salary days. Safer, sure, but not as good for the old retirement fund. This one we got paid all right, considering how easy it was. Kill the crew, take the ship, wait for rendezvous.

"Hey," I asked Jock, "we get cargo salvage on this one?"

"Naw," he replied. Jock had seniority and a few more years in the company than me. He heard stuff I didn't. "Though you could probably take the slug-thrower as a souvenir."

"No thanks," I said, tapping the hard foam on my elbow. "I've already got one souvenir I didn't want."

Four blues lit up inside my bucket. "Friendlies, coming in!" yelled a voice, confirming the computer. We turned to the door as Fire Team Red walked in, which consisted of Corporal Howland, our sometimes medic, plus Privates Ward and Four-Eyes. With them was Master Sergeant Thrasher, aka Squid.

"You boys made a right mess in here," Squid said, looking at the bodies and blood spattered about. "Good work." He noticed my arm. "Tough luck, there, Tommy. That from the slug-thrower?"

"Yeah, Sarge," I replied, as Howland motioned me to sit, then sat down with his bag to take a look at me.

Jock handed the weapon to Squid, who turned it over and examined it closely. "Odd choice for space. Think the owner collected antiques?"

Four-eyes took it from him. "No. This is new," he said. He opened the breech and looked down the barrel. "Probably the first time it was fired."

"Headed for a colony?" Jock suggested.

"Dunno," said the master sergeant. "Not my problem. Find anything interesting in the ship's computer yet, Raymond?"

Raymond, better known as "Four-eyes", had a full AI augment, unlike the rest of us. There were far too many exotic viruses floating around the various planetary nets, to say nothing of the chance of being mind-raped by the devil-gods of the Unity. "Nothing interesting, sir." His face made it obvious he was somewhere else. Probably inside a database. "Cargo is listed as 'industrial, various.'"

"Nice and vague," Squid said. "They wanted it all intact, very pointed on that, so it's probably either weapons or flower arrangements for a royal wedding. We'll come back for a quick look after we hunt down our missing target."

"One left, then," I said.

The master sergeant nodded. "Time to hit engineering. Raymond and Park, you stay here with one-armed Tom. Howland, Ward and Hanley, you're on. Raymond and the rest of you feel free to scan the cargo for items of interest. I just want to make sure we're not dealing with biogenetics or nanites or something that'll trigger Ascendancy interest. We're getting paid good for playing hall monitor."

"Yessir," Four-eyes said mechanically, still far away.

"You're going to live, Tommy," said Howland, putting away his scanner and patting my back. "The joint is fine but you're going to have a heck of a bruise."

"Great," I said, "I'll tell HR that Jock was harassing me."

Park was already walking a row of cargo, helmet off again, looking up and down as he went. Jock and I followed, looking for anything that stood out. Almost everything looked just like the manifest had claimed. Heavy equipment. Parked behind the barrels and shelves were huge grinders and laser augers on treads and various construction equipment I didn't know anything about. I didn't know why the ship was our target and I didn't really care.

I saw some water reclaimers, bundles of piping, spools of wire, lighting, a few ATVs. And then a stack of wooden crates. Wood? What the devil?

"Four-eyes—something strange over here," I said. Wood made no sense.

Four-eyes came. He whistled at the crates. "That is strange," he said, leaning in. "And no maglocks."

"No," said Park, joining us. "We need a crowbar."

Four-eyes looked at him blankly.

"Geez, Four-eyes," I said, "It's a tool. A—"

"A crowbar, wrecking bar, pry bar, or prybar, pinch-bar or sometimes a prise bar, prisebar, and more informally a jimmy, jimmy bar, jemmy or PikiPiki, gooseneck or 'pig foot' is a tool consisting of a metal bar with a single curved end and flattened points, often with a small fissure on one or both ends for removing nails," Four-eyes said, quoting his implant.

"Great, thanks," I said. "Now let's see if we can find something like that."

"We probably shouldn't open them," Four-eyes said, but Park had already returned with a metal bar and jammed it into the gap on the lid of a crate. It popped open easily thanks to the superhuman strength his exo provided. Inside were tightly packed rows of slug guns, wrapped in brown paper and slick with grease.

"Nice," I said. "More antiques."

The next crate was packed with old-style ammunition. Projectiles with chemical propellant.

Park shrugged. "Nothing on the books about old weapons."

"Not our problem," I said, then glanced at the stats. "Fourteen," I said.

As I did, Squid's voice growled over the transceiver. "All clear, gentlemen. Time to clean up."

We left the crates and started dragging bodies to the airlock, Four-eyes leaning over each corpse, his retinal cam storing the data for our client. I got to look at the guy who shot me. He was just a kid, maybe twenty, if that. Well, at least he died fighting. Give him that. The first few guys we took out just ran like rabbits down the corridors.

We unceremoniously stuffed the bodies into the small personnel airlock and flushed them out into space.

"Sergeant Thrasher, cargo is clean," I reported.

"Find anything interesting?"

"Mostly just industrial equipment. Construction stuff," I said. Four-eyes cut in, "To be precise, mining equipment."

"Roger," Squid said. "No problems?"

"Nothing illegal. Some more slug-throwers though, in wood crates," I said.

"Not our business. Everyone meet up on the bridge in five. We've cleared our bodies here, we'll finish there."

"Roger," I replied. Park hammered the tops back on the boxes, then exited cargo. I reset the seals on the door and we headed up to the bridge. It wasn't a huge ship, so no lifts. Just ladders and stairs like an old atomic model.

We entered the bridge just as Private Ward was dragging out the body of the captain. Park saluted the dead man ironically and Jock laughed.

"Now what?" I said.

"Now we wait for a new crew," said Squid from the late captain's chair, a flask in his hand. "Lieutenant says their ship is on the way and they should be here within the hour. At ease for now."

I looked around the bridge. Everything looked clean and well-maintained, though it was an older ship. *Garamond* read the name plate on the wall. *Registration 1001x235htfg22789.113. Gruppo ENIL-EX, Valatesta.*

I took off my helmet and set it on the navigation table next to a personal tablet, still displaying a colorful picture story its owner would never finish. Probably lots of time to read on freighters.

Almost exactly an hour later, a sleek black transport pulled alongside and hailed us. A few moments later, the boarding party joined us. The men wore the same navy blue jumpsuits of the guys we'd just spaced. Gruppo ENIL-EX uniforms, I assumed.

Their leader engaged with Sergeant Thrasher and a severe little man walked up to me. "Do you mind?" he said, then powered up the nav board. He tossed the tablet onto a chair as I gathered up my helmet.

"Good to meet you too," I said, getting out of his way.

"Hmm," he said, keying in some numbers.

"So," I pressed, partly because I was annoyed, "got a hot date, then?"

"Not likely on Ulixis," he sniffed.

"What? You don't like furry chicks?" I remember jokes about the women of Ulixis, though I really only had a vague idea where the place was.

"Go away, Wardog, I'm working," he said, waving his hand dismissively.

I considered shooting him in the back of the head, just on principle, then decided I'd rather not lose my bonus today. Squid didn't take kindly to freelancing.

Chapter 2

Assignment Ulixis

I was wolfing down spaghettini al salvia in the cafeteria when Jock walked in and grabbed a plate of his own. A moment later he joined me, his plate loaded with fish and salad. Around us, dozens of fellow employees sat and ate. Some of them were on-base staffers, others were field operators such as ourselves. Everyone was dressed business casual style, in slacks and collared shirts, but the operators were easy to spot. They were alert and their shirts were tighter, often exposing tattoos as well as various implants and bodymods. I knew most of them, but not all. Wardogs Incorporated is a big operation.

"Carbs will kill you," Jock said, gesturing at my plate. "What the hell is that yellow sauce?"

"Melted butter," I said.

He shook his head. "Just because we have something in the banks doesn't mean you should eat it."

"Shove off," I said. "I eat what I want."

He snorted, then indicated my right arm. "How's the elbow?"

"Better," I said. "Stiff."

"You gotta stretch it," he said.

"Thanks, Mom," I said as I twirled another forkful of sage-and-butter-drenched goodness.

He grinned and attacked his fish. That was one great thing about the private sector, we ate way better than we had back in the military. Some of the mercs from elsewhere in the sector claimed they'd transferred full-time to Kantillon after tasting the food. It was generally agreed that this base had the best. The autochef couldn't make meals out of thin air, not yet, but it did have an impressive bank of food items, deep frozen and ready for assembly at the push of a button.

Park and Four-eyes walked in, trailed by Ward. I waved at them. They made their orders and joined us at the table.

Park, like usual, had ordered a nasty fermented dish, which this time appeared to primarily consist of testicles that had formerly belonged to a quantity of male animals.

"Come on, man!" Jock said. "Take that somewhere we can't smell it. Or see it!"

Park stared at him and without breaking his gaze, speared a misshapen ball, put it in his mouth, chewed deliberately, and swallowed. Jock shivered and went back to his plate of girl food.

Four-eyes ignored the horseplay as he carefully sliced a pork chop into even cubes.

"So, pretty good pay on that last one," Jock changed the subject.

"Yep," I said. "I bought another 150 shares of our stock with it this morning."

"What, didn't you save any for space sirens and cold ones?" Jock said.

"Not me," I said. "I have some credits if I need them. Rather have the money working for me."

"Tom is smart, Jock." Park said approvingly. "If you survive to retire, you'll have nothing but a pension."

"Not me," Jock declared. "Not with all those sugar babies out there looking for a daddy."

"Why would we clear out the civilian crew of a corporate freighter hauling mining equipment?" Four-eyes broke in unexpectedly.

"Clear out?" Ward said. "Dude, we straight-up executed them."

"Whoa, Ward! You going bleeding heart on us?" Jock looked more disgusted than he had over Park's appalling lunch. "They fought back! Just look at Tommy's arm!"

Ward shrugged and pushed a fish stick around his plate. "Those guys tried to defend themselves, sure, but they were just a working ship's crew. Not pirates, not soldiers, not smugglers–"

"That we know of!" Four-eyes broke in.

"They were just normal guys. The last one I killed in engineering wasn't even armed. He was hiding in a janitorial closet. Only 18 or so. Eyed him on the thermal, shot him. Hauled him out, threw him into space."

"Yep," said Jock. "Cha-ching."

Ward shrugged. "Don't seem right."

"Ward," I said, "you're overthinking it. You've killed lots of people. Did all of them deserve it?"

"No," he said.

"See, that's where you're wrong," I said. "Everyone deserves it, sooner or later. No one gets out alive."

Ward shook his head. "I get war. Corporate, territorial, interplanetary, whatever. I don't get this. This was like playing executioner, not soldier. Come on—we took a civilian ship and killed the whole damn crew. What the hell was that?"

"Low-risk profit," Jock said. "The best kind. Hey, you take what you can get. That's the first rule of the space marine: always kill them first. Seriously, though, we were within legal bounds. They had been declared hostile. Don't go turning dime-dropper on us."

"Naw," said Ward, "I won't. Just bugged me, that's all." He took a bite of a fish stick.

He had a point, but when you start identifying with the marks you end by losing your edge. They're targets that emit cash when hit, that's all. And I was serious about people. People suck. Even that nice old lady in the apartment next door probably drowns cats in her bathtub or something. Please punch me in the face if I ever get sentimental over the "innocent." Nobody is innocent.

"Lunch is over," Four-eyes announced. "We've got a briefing."

"Oh, come on," Jock said. "Already? We just got back."

Four-eyes was already walking to the recycler as the notification hit my wristband. Four-eyes' AI was always a few seconds ahead. Unlike a lot of guys, I didn't stay jacked 24/7. I saved it for missions. As I dumped my plate in the recycler, I noticed it wasn't just our squad getting called—the rest of the mercs in the room were clearing, leaving behind the pencil-necks and office girls.

And we'd been summoned to the auditorium, not a conference room. Big thing, then. I hoped it was a raise announcement but probably not. Probably some corporate nonsense about new tax forms.

I took a seat in our company's assigned seating. Middle right of the auditorium. Squid was already there, along with Ace and Four-eyes. Most of the 120 seats assigned to Kilo Company weren't filled as multiple platoons were out on missions, but the Bastards were present. That's my platoon. Best damn bunch of killers in the galaxy. We waited at attention, catching eyes and shrugging, wondering what the deal could be. Captain Marks's seat was designated at the back of us, but he walked forward and whispered a few words to Squid before taking his position. I saw the master sergeant raise his eyebrows, then shake his head. Jock and Park were towards the back, and I saw Ward towards the front, gnawing a fingernail, obviously still thinking about our last mission.

In a few more minutes the lights dimmed. I looked around the three-thousand-seat auditorium. There were probably four hundred men present. Not bad for an impromptu briefing on such short notice.

Purvis Whittaker, the VP of Operations, took the stage without fanfare. He was accompanied by another man I didn't recognize, though he also wore a general's uniform. We stood at attention as they entered.

"Good afternoon, men," said General Whittaker, returning our salutes. "Good news. We've got a nice fat contract for you all." He squinted out towards the audience. "At ease. Sit down, this is going to take a little while," he said, waving us down. "We've got our first real big job of the year, a solid private contract, and you're all invited. I'm not going to tell you about it, though. Here with me is a man most of you probably haven't served with. General Dex Hampton. He's going to lay out your mission. Dex is VP of sales and marketing in the Kantillon subsector and nailed down this gig for you boys. All yours, General."

Whittaker strode back and took a chair on the stage as Hampton nodded and addressed us. He was tall, with slick black hair.

"Good day, men. We have signed a contract pledging an entire regiment to an action which will take place on Ulixis."

A murmur went around the room. Entire regiments were only contracted occasionally, as the expense was huge. And Ulixis, I thought, that was where the freighter had–

"The Empire of Ulimba-Mor needs our services against their neighbor and rival, the Kingdom of Corwistal," the general continued. "The monarchies are two of the four hundred eighteen states presently extant on Ulixis, which, as you know if you brushed up on your astronavigation, is the only habitable planet in the system. The empire is attempting to regain some valuable territory it lost five decades ago so the emperor himself has decided to hire the very best, and of course, we are pleased to be of service.

"This is not an optional mission and all leaves are canceled. You have twenty-seven hours to tie up loose ends before you ship out."

I saw surprise on a lot of faces and a lot of whistles and exclamations of surprise. That was a fast turnaround. Had to be some serious money involved in this one. A whole regiment too!

The general took out a small tablet from his pocket and touched it, projecting a large holographic image of the planet over his head.

"You're going here," he said, and the image zoomed in towards a stubby peninsula on the edge of one of the continents. Far above it was the border of the Ulimbese empire. Their territory was marked in purple, but a stabbing yellow and purple striped region dove down to the peninsula, which was deep inside the sprawling yellow of the Kingdom of Corwistal. An X blinked on the peninsula.

"You will help the Ulimbese secure the peninsula for the emperor, remaining until all resistance has been neutralized and our client signs off. This shouldn't be a tough one for you, as, frankly, the Kingdom of Corwistal cannot field troops with anything near your level of experience or training.

"I should let you know, however, that not all of you are going to have a good time, especially those of you who spend most of your time jacked.

"Ulixis is a tech level 10 planet, so—"

A groan rounded the room at this point.

"It sounds like most of you already know the drill. No advanced implants, no AI drones, no powered armor, no plasma rifles." The general was reading from a list now. "External communications only, projectile weapons, optical sights, simple remote-controlled drones. Think of it as experiencing living history."

I'd had to do a TL-12 world before, but a tech level of 10 was practically stone age. I looked at my bandaged elbow. Fighting without an exo-suit promised for some crazy stuff.

"And, of course, you'll be getting daily combat-rate," General Hampton continued. "Regardless of whether you see combat that day or not. Squads and companies will stay together, though this is a short-notice operation, so there will be some personnel substitutions. On a related matter, those of you with implants will need keep in mind that the Ascendancy doesn't allow for higher-rated devices, even if they are medically necessary."

I saw Squid swear under his breath. The sergeant was by far our most experienced soldier in the squad, but there were rumors that he had at least one artificial organ.

"Most of your records are documented, of course, so don't think you're going to sneak onto the operation with anything fancier than a titanium knee. Recuse yourself now and sit this one out. Also, everyone's getting scanned. If they spy so much as a digital lymph node that we don't already know about, your ass is grass. And by grass, I mean kicked off the operation and fined. Got it?"

A chorus of "yes sirs," echoed through the room. I would be in. Four-eyes would have to unplug, but I thought he'd be good to go. Rest of the guys, so far as I knew, would be in.

"Excellent," said General Hampton. "Other than the tech limits, you guys are going to have a good time. The Apis Peninsula is a moderately prosperous region known for its wine production, as well as sheep, rum cherries, and attractive young women of questionable morals. It's also the winter residence of the King of Corwistal, as seen here." The map zoomed in on an estate. "This is outside our range of objectives, but it is indeed the winter there right now, though we have no idea if any of the royal family were in the region during the latest push by the Ulimbese. Not our problem, though. Our job is to secure the area under the direction of the Ulimbese, reinforcing their push and holding the ground they've established.

"Despite the winter, the weather on the surface right now is mild. Air might be a little thick for some of you, but it doesn't even get near freezing at night. Great weather for war—like taking a vacation. Have a rum cherry cocktail for me once you get our client settled, okay boys? This is a great chance to do the company proud, and if we pull around a job like this on such short notice, I can almost guarantee that just the news that we have been able to deliver so quickly on this scale is going to give our stock bump. Lots of you guys are holding WDI long-term, so consider this a nice boost for your retirement funds as well as a good chunk of cash right now."

There was a mild murmur of amusement. The sales guys weren't our favorite employees in the operation, but it had to be said, they did bring in the loot.

"Thank you, men. That's all I have for you for now. I'll let General Whittaker wrap things up." General Hampton pushed a button and Ulixis disappeared.

General Whittaker stood and Hampton took his place behind him.

"Okay, men. We're going to have to activate some reservists and bring on a few short-term contractors, but we will deliver a full regiment on schedule, even with those of you with implants being disqualified. At approximately this time tomorrow, you will be transported into orbit to rendezvous with the KCS *Ridgeback*, a combat-ready starcruiser that we have rented from the Kantillonese Navy for the delivery just in case hostiles attempt to interfere with our transit. We've used her before, she's a good ship, with a veteran crew. The *Ridgeback* will remain in orbit for another 24-hour period until the entire regiment is on board. It will then jump to Feymanus, then Faraday, then a quick hop to Ulixis. You should be there in 72 hours from now. I recommend you spend your time jacked in and learning what you can about the locals and the terrain, as well as re-familiarizing yourself with projectile weapons and dumb armor.

"Those of you with tech certs need to make sure you're up on your external communications and drones. Get going on the simulations now, and also make sure you rest up. Just because the general here thinks this will be a cakewalk, remember he's a sales guy first. He's going to give you the good news. Don't get cocky. Even though these guys are medieval, remember that a bullet can kill a man just as dead as a plasma bolt. That is all. Go get ready, men. And good luck."

After the generals left the stage, we all stood up and I made my way over to catch Squid but he had already walked out. Jock and Park caught me before I hit the aisle.

"Ready for a vacation, Tommy?" Jock grinned.

"Sure, you got some tickets to Rhysalan? I think I'll hit a few casinos and pick up a chick with tentacles."

"No, this mission, jackass," Jock said. "It's going to be cake."

Park nodded. "Easy one, most def."

"Yeah, no worries here. I'm gonna miss my targeting and thermals, though. Not to mention my rifle."

"Sure," Jock said, "but it's almost like getting back to nature. Wild and free. Man vs. man, just primitive weapons, blue sky above, no pulse weapons or disrupters–"

"I like disrupters," I said. "No mess."

"Not when they're aimed at you," Park pointed out.

"No, that's true." Then I noticed Private Ward, sitting lost in thought. Jock caught my glance. "Yeah, he's philosophizing. Are you philosophizing, Ward?" he said louder, slapping the back of his head.

Ward frowned and turned. "No. I'm thinking."

"About those poor innocent lambs we knocked off?" Jock needled.

"No," said Ward. "I'm just wondering what's going on with Ulixis. It's an agricultural planet.

"Land grab, kid," I said to him. "One guy wants something the other guy has, so we take it for him."

"Yeah, I get that," he said, "but I served five years in the orbital patrol here on Kantillon before signing on with WDI. Nothing is ever quite that simple. Sure, the way it's sold, one guy wants us to fight another. Does the news ever get that sort of thing right? No. So who knows what's really going on? A fast turnaround for a whole regiment? Seems to lack a certain level of planning for a contract that size. Or there's something shady behind it and the money at stake has to be ridiculous. What kind of backwater monarch could pull this off just to take a peninsula?"

"Dunno," I said. "Mining rights, probably. Maybe it's made of solid gold or something."

I slapped him on the shoulder and walked out. Overthinking the contract wasn't my thing. Show up, shoot, and get paid. That was more my style.

I caught up with Squid later. As I assumed, he was out on the barracks balcony, smoking a cigar. He loved his cigars, but he had to go without whenever we were in space. So naturally, every time we got back to base or were out dirtside, he'd fire up a stogie.

"Sergeant," I greeted him.

"Hey Tommy. Aren't you supposed to be learning how to use a slingshot or something?"

"Already did enough of that for one day," I said. I'd run through a hundred rounds and decided I was already pretty damn good with the Katzers they were issuing us. There was nothing to them. They were projectile rifles with a 475 mm barrel that fired a 5.5x50 cartridge to an effective range of 450 meters. No assisted targeting, no digitals, they were little more than a slingshot that went bang and threw a very small stone. "So, you not coming?"

Squid spit. "Nope."

"Dammit, Sergeant—the Bastards need you!"

Squid took a deep puff and blew a smoke ring. Then he shook his head. "Not up to me, Tommy. You heard the man. And Jock will do fine as squad leader. He knows his head from his ass. I recommended him myself."

I shrugged. "So it's true what they say. You do have a robo-penis."

He laughed dryly. "Nah, but I'm DQ'd on four counts."

"Four?" I repeated, surprised.

"Four." He took his finger and tapped it directly on his open left eye with a highly unnatural clicking sound. "That, for one. Could have it taken out for the mission, of course, but that's not the problem."

He pulled up his shirt to reveal three faint white lines converging over his bellybutton. "Got that done on the field, ergo the scars."

"Liver?" I ventured. He nodded, then took another deep draw on his cigar, then exhaled slowly, blowing another smoke ring in the air. Here in the midst of flexicrete and transparent aluminum buildings, the wind was blocked, allowing the "O" to hang in the air and disintegrate slowly.

"And both of these," he said at long last, thumping his chest. "Burned out in a raid. Bucket filter failed and I got a good lungful of some kind of burning neo-foam. Burned like acid. They had to put me in a gelpack that time. It was close, but I made it. So, they hooked me up with a pair of artificials. Not bad, really. Supposed to deliver 25 percent more oxygen than the originals. Best part is that I don't have to worry about lung cancer no more."

"But you're out of the game now," I said.

"Yeah, for this one, anyhow," he said. "Look, Tommy, you just listen to Jock, don't get yourself killed and we'll be back raiding freighters and murdering civilians for profit in no time." He pulled a bottle from his jacket and took a swig. I thought he was going to offer it to me, but instead, he slapped me on the shoulder. "Get out of here, kid."

I nodded and turned to leave, but as I opened the door to go back inside, he spoke again.

"Tommy?"

"Yeah?" I said, turning back to face him.

"Watch your back. These big contracts, when they go south, they tend to go south in a big way."

Chapter 3

Assault at Apis

I looked out the windows of the shuttle as we got close to the ship, not caring to play it cool like some of the guys. I'd always loved space and I'd always loved warships, and I wasn't going to miss a chance to see a classic. The *Ridgeback* hung in orbit over Kantillon, lit up blood-red by light of the sun shining through the atmosphere, looking just like the model I'd had as a kid. It was a *Vladivos*-class starcruiser design which had remained almost unchanged for five decades. Bristling with lasers, EMP pulse cannons and long-range smart torpedoes, plus reactors large enough to power a moon and space in her belly for a multiple troop transports, she was more than able to deal with any fighters or pirates that might threaten our safe passage to Ulixis.

There was a shuddering clang as our transport docked with the *Ridgeback*, then a hiss of equalizing pressure and the swish of an opening airlock.

Needless to say, the trip to Ulixis was uneventful. We mostly played cards, and I lost a month's pay to Four-Eyes. Even if someone had gotten wind of our mission and wanted to interfere with it, no one in their right mind was going to mess with a *Vladivos*-class cruiser.

We hit orbit and loaded onto our armored transport by troop and company. Our armored ground vehicles would be following in a second craft, right after us. Our space-to-ground troop transport was an old school chunky behemoth, with all of us strapped in rows and rows. This Tech 10 thing was messing with my head, but it was a helluva lot better than the *Lightning*-class transports. I'll take walking off of a ship over being fired out of it like a champagne cork any day. I sat between Jock and Four-eyes, who was looking strangely attentive without his AI to keep him company. Everyone loaded efficiently, level by level, company by company; 30 companies, 3600 mercs total, plus at least another 500 support personnel, all heading down to the surface. We were suited up in our dumb armor and uniforms, baggage stowed under the seat in front of us. Like passengers on a spaceliner, except they weren't stowing rifles and packs under the seats. And no cute stewardesses.

CLANG—CLUNK—I heard the transport disengage and begin its fall to the planet, like a big tortoise. No antigrav on this thing. My stomach flopped as we left the *Ridgeback's* field, then started our descent through the atmosphere to the planetary surface, the big transport engines kicking in to control our gravity-assisted fall.

There are no windows on an armored transport, for obvious reasons, so it felt rather like being strapped inside a big trashcan. The pressure in my ears made it hard to hear, so when I heard the first impact I thought it was just turbulence. Then there was another impact. Park swore and thumped me in the ribs. "We're taking fire!" he yelled.

"Fire?" I yelled back. "They said we were supposed to be landing in friendly territory!"

THWACK! Something hit us like a punch in the face, rocking the ship violently. The lights dimmed for a second as we swung about. My head jerked back and my chest hit the straps so hard it felt like they'd cut my chest. "We're going in hot!" someone yelled. We ducked into defensive crouches in our seats as best as we could and waited…then I heard the most beautiful sound in the world. The crack of thunder!

"It's the cruiser! Listen! That sound is lasers burning through the atmosphere!" Jock cheered.

He was right. It wasn't the transport ship, which was armored, but wasn't armed. It was the mighty *Ridgeback*. *CRACK! CRACK!* There were multiple concussions as the ship's powerful targeting AI's tracked incoming missiles and fried their sensors before they could hit us. *CRACK!* What a beautiful sound! I don't know if the captain of the *Ridgeback* figured being outside the atmosphere gave him immunity to the planetary tech regulations or if he figured that he could get away with it so long as he stuck to defensive measures, but I didn't care. I was just really glad I wasn't going to get blown apart with my friends inside a perforated tin can.

The transport captain had no choice but to go in fast and hard. When I felt us slam down to the ground and heard the hiss of the settling hydraulics, I finally took a breath again. My relief didn't last long, though. I could hear the pinging of small arms fire and the thump of mortars even from inside the armored ship.

"Great," Jock muttered. "Nothing like a hot LZ. Looks like our hosts aren't quite as friendly as we thought they were."

We unstrapped ourselves, grabbed our packs and Katzers, and waited for the company in front of us to debark. We were next. Then "Ears in, boys! Now!" yelled Captain Marks and we complied. The earpieces were devices that hooked around the ear and you had a box on your chest that was the radio itself. You actually had to depress a switch to talk. Ridiculous! We hadn't even seen the colonel running this operation yet. I figure he'd been sent ahead, along with some support guys. Then his voice came over the radio. He sounded pretty chill, which helped calm my frazzled nerves.

"Listen up, Wardogs. Colonel Emerson here. Looks like they had a welcome party waiting for us. Stay cool and we will get this all sorted. 1st and 2nd Battalions, head directly to the southern perimeter and assist the Ulimbese units now defending it. 3rd, 4th, and 5th Battalions, you will unload the incoming transport and defend the ships. We need that gear yesterday. Work with local ground ops— and get a move on!"

We were in the 2nd Battalion, which put us in the line of fire. That suited me just fine. I was ready to give my antique of a rifle a working-in and would rather take the fight to the enemy than pick up heavy

stuff and put it down somewhere else, especially if that involved being
shot at.

It was dark outside and everything was a confusing mess as we
headed down the long ramp to the ground. The landing zone was
a flurry of activity. Men swarmed around the bottom of the transport, pulling out crates of ammo, food and various supplies. Our
surroundings looked as if we were inside what had been some sort
of a resort, now turned amateur military base. Razor wire and thick
armor panels were thrown up around the edges, a few large projectile guns pointed skywards, a dozen haphazardly parked land vehicles
were scattered about, while men in severe black uniforms with red
trim—presumably our Ulimbese allies—were alternatively shouting
directions and arguing with our guys.

Like I said, it was a mess. When we hit the ground, Captain Marks
lit up a baton and we followed him. He had the map, we had the
firepower, so all we had to do was get stuck in where we were needed,
then hold.

CRACK! A mortar of some kind nailed the side of the transport and
exploded, failing to pierce the armor but knocking a half dozen men
off one of the ramps. I'm sure it killed at least two of them. I'd just
been standing there less than two minutes before. Damn!

When we hit the ground we only had our Katzers, torso armor,
helmets, and backpacks containing ammo and basic supplies. No
heavy weapons, grenades or mortars. I don't think much more than
food and ammo was jammed in the bottom of the transport. The
air was cool but not cold, the gentle breeze contrasting with crackle
of small arms fire and the thumping of mortars. Men unpacked and
the less-than-half of Kilo company that had made it to Ulixis followed
Captain Marks. As we jogged with him to wherever he was taking us, I
heard the sound of a jet above, then the rattle of a massive anti-aircraft
gun spitting fire from somewhere inside the enclosure. That was the
last aircraft I heard that evening—for all I know, it might have been
some tycoon heading off to greener pastures.

Jock told me the second transport would soon deliver our vehicles, including tanks, cannon, extra drones, additional food, ammo, mines and other goodies. Once they showed up, we'd be able to conquer the entire peninsula in an afternoon, should the brass decide to.

We got to the edge of the camp where the big metal chunks of wall stood like looming gray dominos in the night. They looked like they'd been ripped off the side of an antique aircraft carrier. One of them even had some faded remnants of numbers painted on on the side. Scaffolding had been put behind them, with embrasures, a few of which held Ulimbese snipers. Judging from the sound of the battle, we were maybe a mile or two behind the heavy fighting.

"Okay men, here's the deal," Captain Marks barked over the noise. "Out there we've got a line of battle being held by multiple Ulimbese armored divisions. They have been unable to prevent the establishment of multiple mortar teams, plus they're telling me they think there are big guns and armor coming in for a full assault on the base itself. We're going to go by squads and spread out, aiming for maximum damage to advancing enemy. Two in each squad will carry RPGs with two extra rounds on their person, with two men in the team acting as their support, each individual carrying rifles and four additional RPG rounds, then a sniper and a spotter, plus the team leader. Use what you can for cover, stay low, spread out and get the bastards." We had six squads. Marks and a lieutenant stayed behind to work strategy.

Park was sniper as always, and Jock put Four-eyes on an RPG, giving the other RPG to a guy I hadn't met before, recently assigned to our company with a stellar background in the military. Corporal Jones. Serious guy, black hair. I was glad I didn't get a grenade launcher. Sure, they were fun to shoot on a range but were unwieldy as hell in action and gave you almost no self-defense against guys with rifles, unless you went center-mass on a guy. That wasn't the way to win bonus bucks. Private Ward got RPG backup duty for the serious guy, and Private Leighton got backup on Four-eyes. I was a spotter for Park and Rocky—more properly called Corporal Joe Cellucci—was on machine gun. Rocky was a grinning, bald SOB who loved combat. He was never happier than when someone was shooting at him.

It took us a few moments to get our gear set, then we headed beyond the armor plate wall and into the countryside, followed by Bastard Squad 2, and Raptor Platoon Squads 1 and 2, while the remaining two Kilo Company squads—Homewrecker Platoon—got deployed from another point.

My night vision goggles worked well, despite the antique design. Just outside the makeshift walls of the base was what had been a very nice sweeping lawn and parking lot, now pocked and burnt and rutted. By the parking lot was a shattered building, broken windows and bricks. Off to the right was a tree-lined road. A sign about 400 meters out read something in a local language that looked like spitballs to me. It featured a pretty woman eating a sandwich. Restaurant ad, maybe for the smashed building. I noted she wasn't furry. If we ever got a break, it would be interesting to do some independent field research on the local ladies.

Other teams from other companies streamed out behind us, heading for points all across the map. Jones took point for our squad, leading us quickly past the destroyed building. Glass crunched beneath my boots and I smelled rotting food. Yep, restaurant. Up ahead loomed dark woods and undeveloped country. The terrain was mostly rolling hills, the kind that loop and roll up and then down into little valleys with streams, the real shape of the topography softened and obscured by trees. We entered a patch of woods which turned out to be less dense than I'd feared once we got under the canopy. The leaves beneath our feet smelled richly of fungi, mixed with the smoke. If it weren't for the sounds of battle, we could be completely alone here. Just some guys walking in the woods. With night vision, armor and RPGs. Damn, what I wouldn't have given for some Wardog armor. Or a few missile crews. They weren't even here and we were heading out. Sending infantry to battle tanks felt like a desperation move—but we'd had no time to prep.

We moved slowly, coming closer and closer to the sound of battle, scanning as we went. I was on point when we made first contact with the enemy. *CRACK!* A bullet snapped into a tree—right next to my helmet! I hit the ground like a rock and the rest of the team did as well.

"Give me eyes! Where'd that come from?" Jock hissed into his radio.

I looked but saw nothing but the thermal signatures of my team, plus some small animals and birds, scattered here and there.

CRACK! To the left! I jerked my head over and saw the edge of a figure peeking around a tree, maybe 300 yards out. "Got him, Sergeant—4 o'clock," I said, but Rocky and some others were already spraying rounds. The outline disappeared—he's staying behind a tree, a big one. Back home I'd say it's a 300-year-old monster. Lots of cover. Rocky saw that too and stopped shooting. Park was already crawling out for a clear shot, then there was another shot from off somewhere and I see the enemy fall down next to the tree on the thermal. Someone hit him, but wasn't us. Then the radio crackled again. "Friendlies coming up on your position to the right."

"Acknowledged. Good timing," Jock says, getting up from the ground, then turning to us. "Okay, everyone, keep your eyes out for thermals so we don't miss their infantry screen. They probably aren't dumb enough to lead with their armor."

I realized the terrain had brought our squads together, the more open ridges on either side of the forested valley likely narrowing towards the battle.

We moved ahead catlike, coming up towards the sound of battle. As we got closer, the trees above lit up with bursts of light like lightning, as shells exploded and scattered the shadows. And then we came to the smoldering edge of the forest and looked out into a hell of burning vehicles, fallen men, churning armor and flaming fuel. A convoy of Ulimbese armored assault vehicles were pinned down in the valley, facing across a creek towards a high position with a road wrapping around the waist of a mountainside.

"What the hell?" Jock said over the radio. "They don't even seem to have any armor! How did they pin 'em?"

As he said it, I caught a glimpse of two trucks zipping around the mountain road on the other side, loaded with men. Corwistalian troops. Then there was a massive *Thump-CRACK!* as a Ulimbese tank exploded while climbing the other side.

"Artillery!" someone snapped. "Big stuff!"

Judging by the size of the explosions, they were firing at least 100mm shells. And it wasn't just the artillery. The Corwistalians must have had fire teams scattered throughout the woods. I saw a streak of fire come down and into the armored division, taking the tread off another tank. And then another *Thump-CRACK!* of a shell. Farther along the mountain, they had a cannon and had pinned them in nicely.

I was starting to get the picture here—the Ulimbese had pushed forward, expecting to face minimal resistance, only to have been pinned at the worst possible point by a well-positioned Corwistalian force. Behind me I heard the thunder of a large ship taking off and looked back towards the landing zone in time to see our troop transport heading back for the safety of space. I fought the sinking wave of despair that briefly threatened to overwhelm me.

It was one thing to go planetside knowing that you could get off any time you liked. But considering how much heat we had taken coming in, I knew there was no guarantee that we would be able to get off again easily.

Captain Marks's voice came over the radio, calm and collected. "Wardogs, our allies need an infantry screen. Advance and neutralize the enemy anti-tank teams."

We immediately advanced into the woods, moving to follow it around and across the creek farther upstream, then come down. Even now, other squads were scaling the ridge to the other side. Ulimbese snipers and light mortars were firing into the woods ahead of us anytime they got a bead on a source of incoming fire, and I sincerely hoped they would keep their targeting well ahead of our advance.

The terrain was rough and the trees went from dense to patchy as rocks pushed up in shelves and bumps along the hillside. The going was slow until we came across an access road. Probably a farm lane. It was muddy in some spots and rutted with truck tracks, in between areas where boulders had been smashed down to flatten the passage. Then we reached a metal bridge over a ravine. The creek rushed below, wild between the rocks. If the Ulimbese had been more careful, they could have brought their armor through up here—but it was a linear danger area and a good place to get nailed. We stopped and got eyes on the woods, seeing nothing. The bridge wasn't a long stretch, but it was wide open.

"Cellucci and Ward, secure the opposite side!" Jock ordered, and they did, running across quickly before covering the woods. Four-eyes and Jock went next, then Jones and Leighton, then finally, it was time for Park and me to cross.

We moved fast and low, then the next squad started once we were clear. They were about halfway across when I saw a blast of fire from the woods and an RPG streak up from a little below in the ravine. It just missed the bridge and arced across into the woods. *CRACK!* A tree exploded into flames and plummeted down into the creek. The rest of the men on the other side took defensive positions and started pumping suppressive fire into the woods where the grenade had emerged.

"Get down there and nail that RPG team!" Jock yelled, and we cut through the woods, trying to get eyes on the enemy. Even with our thermals the trees were dense here. I went in a beeline with Park as some of the other men cut around. My chest pounded as we found a small clearing I assumed was the spot where they'd launched.

Park and I searched the location, seeing nothing…nothing…nothing—then I saw something out of the corner of my eye—a hand on a trunk! I opened fire and the man ran, dropping his launcher and followed by a second soldier. Park nailed the second one through the back as I blasted at the second guy. He went down hard. "We got them, Sergeant," I reported as I came up on the bodies. Park's guy was dead, but the guy I hit was still alive and bleeding from a wound on his thigh.

"Shoot," I said to Park. "I'm still getting used to these old rifles. I suppose we could tie that leg off, then we could–"

CRACK! Park shot the wounded man in the head.

"...or we could just do that," I said.

"Friendlies incoming!" came a voice. Cellucci, approaching with Jones.

"You see any more?" I asked them and Rocky shook his head.

"This was it," Park said, rooting through one of the dead men's clothes and coming out with a knife. He pulled it from its sheath and tried the edge, grinned, then stuck it in his pack.

"RPG neutralized, Sergeant," I reported in over the com. "We are returning to the bridge."

When we got back the rest of the squads were already over. We entered the woods on the other side and left the road, dividing in two and following it through the woods. It was slower, but running down an open road is a great way to end up shot to pieces. Then—headlights ahead!

We hit the ground, trusting our camo and the night to hide us. The vehicle zipped past, another truck with four men in the back. One guy held an RPG, the others rifles. The side of the truck had a basket of roots painted on it, along with some of their spitball text. Farm truck. Damn kids had spirit.

"Hit 'em, Raymond!" Jock hissed, but another squad member was already in the road with his RPG, launching a grenade after the retreating vehicle. The explosion was incredible—he must have hit the fuel tank. No way anyone survived THAT. Jones and Cellucci ran over to confirm the kills, then gave us the thumbs up.

We kept advancing, moving toward where we'd seen the anti-tank teams targeting the Ulimbese armor. At that point, our squads split up.

Jock went ahead with the rest of the team, while Park went up a tree with his rifle as I watched the ground. If the enemies had infrared, Park was a sitting duck. If they didn't, they were sitting ducks. Our RPG teams moved to clear locations to watch for fire.

I couldn't see a thing except Park above and some sort of an owl up a tree about 10 paces to the left. It was picking at its feathers calmly, just as if the locals weren't blasting and burning the living crap out of its neighborhood. Retard.

Somewhere ahead I again heard the thump of heavy cannon. We'd be able to take the teams in the woods, I was sure, but the cannon might not be easily accessible.

I looked up at Park, who had his rifle to his eye. He sighted in, and squeezed off a round. The muzzle flash was suppressed but I could see it on my thermal.

Then I took a bullet in the back—what the HELL! It had gone right through my pack and buried itself in my armor. I spun and opened up with my rifle and went low, not seeing anything but sure as hell not going to just stand there and look around while he sighted in on my throat. Or my elbow.

Two men—crouching, a boulder in front of them. I hooked a grenade out of my belt, popped the pin and winged it, seeing them scramble as it swished into the brush between them. Not fast enough! POW! My vision lit up white as the grenade exploded, then cleared. One of the two was down, the other, hopping through the brush. I tagged him twice with my rifle and he went down.

"You okay?" Park whispered over the radio.

"Yeah, just having a cuppa tea down here. You keep enjoying your tree."

He said nothing as he sighted in again. I dropped my damaged pack on the ground, only to feel it come away thick and sticky. Blood? I hunched low and checked quickly, then breathed a sigh of relief. The slug had gone right through a lasagna MRE. Probably ruined the pound cake, too. I dropped the mess and got back up, keeping my back to the tree and eyeing the woods.

A couple of minutes later, Park came down from above. "Let's move on—resistance is mostly gone here." I snatched up my mess of a pack and put it back on my back. So much for dinner.

THUMP—the sound of cannon came echoing again. They had been firing about a shell a minute for the last ten minutes. "Moving out," Park radioed to Jock, "approaching your position." He pulled out his GPS tablet. I hadn't been issued one, but was glad to see his. We had a scattering of our guys across the mountainside and Park quickly ID'd the location of our squad.

As we pressed forward through the woods we came to a rocky opening on the hillside and I could see the battlefield, now from the other side. It was obvious that the Ulimbese had been cocky, attempting to bring their armored division straight through over the creek in the hollow. I saw that a few tanks had made it across and were directing fire upwards towards a far-off ridge. Then there was a flash from the ridge and I realized that was where the enemy cannon must be stationed.

"No way we'll make it up there," Park said. "And those tanks can't hit there from here—too far."

I wished we could call in an orbital bombardment at that point, vaporizing the enemy guns. It could never be easy.

We came up on Jock and the boys a few minutes later. They were watching the armored column from above. More of them had made it across the creek and the wrecks caused by the enemy anti-tank teams had been cleared. We'd opened it up, but *THUMP-CRACK!*—even as we watched, a tank was brewed up on our side of the river when a high-explosive shell struck its turret. There was no way they were going to make it all the way into the next town, even without the threat of RPGs. The Corwistalian artillery was sighted in, they had a clear shot down into the valley, and could drop HE on us all night long if they had the ammo for it.

Marks's voice came over the radio. "Sitrep?"

"The anti-tank teams are neutralized, sir," Jock said, "but that artillery on the hillside is doing a number on the friendly armor."

"Can you reach them?"

"Negative, sir. Way out of range."

There was a silence for a moment, as if the captain were in conference with someone else.

"Sit tight," he said at long last. "We're going to drone 'em."

If you've ever been hunted by an AI drone, you know it's no picnic. I'd rather face a charging Mephistan blood hog than go eye to eye with a killer robot. Those bastards have everything from venom needles to sonic weapons to macerating blades, in the case of the nasty Mk. II terror mods. But these drones weren't like that—they were some sort of old-tech dumb drones. A guy actually sat somewhere with a joystick and controlled the thing, pressing buttons to shoot or punching in a kill code to trigger kamikaze mode for those armed with explosives.

We sat in silence, watching the skies for what seemed like an hour, and all the while the booming thump of the cannon sounded, over and over, taking out too many of our allies.

And then we saw them, black against the deep sky, long wings making the stars blink in and out. One, then another, heading towards that ridge. Deadly quiet, high above. I remembered that model. They could fire missiles or be used as a flying bomb. Since we couldn't paint the target with lasers to allow a smart strike, I was guessing they would do the latter.

The night suddenly fell quiet and it stayed that way for a little while. The cannons had quit firing. Were they out of ammunition? I peered toward the ridge and magnified. I could just make out the gun's barrel. Then I saw the muzzle flash, and a few seconds later heard the deep booming sound roll over the hills. And then there was another crack. They had two stationed there, I realized.

The volley did nothing that I could tell. I couldn't see the drones anymore but they had to be almost over their targets. The cannons fired again, and then there was an big explosion that wasn't gunfire. A moment later, it was followed by another!

"YEEEEEEEAH! We got 'em!" someone yelled over the radio. I saw Rocky pump his fist and Jock slapped me on the back.

And then, just when I thought we'd shut them down, I saw more lights approaching from inside Corwistalian territory. They'd be here in perhaps twenty minutes.

"Back to base, 1st—now!" came Colonel Emerson's voice over the radio. "We've got a situation here. 2nd, you will reinforce the Ulimbese armor and help them hold off the enemy assault."

"Captain?" Jock said on Marks's channel. "What's going on back there? We've got some incoming here too."

The radio crackled and hissed and it took a moment, then Marks came on the line. "Under…attack here, got a problem, too. Big problem. Get back! Watch for tanks, watch for–" and then there was a pop, followed by dead air.

"Captain!" Jock said. "Captain—do you read? Do you read?"

Nothing but empty static.

"Let's git!" Jock said and we started back towards base, meeting up with men as we did. We passed Park's tree and that stupid owl was still sitting over there. Maybe he was the smart one.

We reached the bridge, still intact—thank space—and we met more of our men there, and then, as we got to the edge of the woods, we could see the wrecked restaurant sitting silent like a beached leviathan. Clear, but we could hear the pitched sounds of battle from beyond the teeth of the armored wall of the base. We fell back as fast as we could, flooding in through the rear of the base. Looking around. I saw no sign of Captain Marks anywhere, but the place was a madhouse. We had mortars coming in overhead from the opposite side.

"The fun never ends!" Rocky yelled at me. "They must've come in from the other side while we were out in the woods." He picked up a fallen machine gun, checked the magazine, winked and headed across.

I tossed my damaged pack on the ground against a pillar and took a swig from my canteen, then left the pack and went to the other side. On the way I caught a worried Ulimbese infantryman by the arm. "Hey," I said, "what's happening?"

"Corwie assault on the east flank. Hey, weren't you guys were supposed to bring in more armor?"

"Yeah, it should be here."

"No," he shook his head. "I didn't see any. Hey, I gotta run!"

What the hell? Our armor was supposed to have landed right behind us. Where was it? The second transport was also carrying most of our rations, ammo, our big guns, sheesh—even pre-fab buildings, not to mention field hospital supplies. Where in the damn system was it?

The rattling of small arms fire was intense—the air above my head was thick with bullets, but I was protected by the armored plates.

I reached the wall to defend against the assault and looked out at a mess of vehicles and men, moving in from the woods and from behind buildings. Some of our boys raced to try and take a position on the field behind an outbuilding, but a bouncing grenade round exploded over their heads, knocking them to the ground, in what state I don't know. The others were methodically picked off by sniper fire. Meanwhile, they were pounding in mortars behind us. Without heavy guns, we weren't in a good shape.

Then Jock came up behind me. "Tommy, we got bad news."

"No armor," I said.

He nodded. "The second transport never showed. No armor, no nothing."

"Did it get shot down?"

"Nobody knows anything. Except it's not here."

"Can we at least get some drones up?" I asked. If nothing else, we should be able to see what we're facing. Maybe even find the wreck of the transport and salvage something from it.

"Scuttlebutt is the techs are putting together some anti-tank mods. They're improvising, should be back up soon."

"Oh, come on! We shouldn't be hunkering down. We should be kicking ass! These Corwies are barely more than a sub-planetary militia!" I waved my hand towards the field in frustration.

Then the colonel's voice came over the radio, calm and clear. "Just hold the perimeter, men, and keep your heads down. We have Ulimbese air coming in behind us. Sit tight and wait upon your platoon leader's command. We'll follow up on the aerial assault; they won't be prepared for that."

That was a relief. I took a position and looked for targets, popping off rounds at anything that moved, though probably doing nothing more than making them think twice about getting closer. And then, from the north, the gunships came swooping in low over the trees. They looked like clunky vultures of death, with dual rotors and dual machine guns pointing forward from their missile-bearing bellies.

The enemy had seen them and started firing upwards, but the gunships had a long range, launching missiles down towards the Corwistalian troops. Explosion after explosions rocked the field and then I saw the enemy break and flee, trucks, men on foot—all racing back into the woods.

"Move out!" the captain ordered, and we tore out the gates and after the retreating Ulimbese, firing as we leapfrogged forward. Overhead, the gunships shredded the forest ahead of us. I ran past bodies on the ground. I pressed into the woods and saw a guy in front of me throw down his RPG and spring over a drainage ditch. I hit him mid-jump and he crumpled. I saw Rocky to my left clubbing a fallen Corwie with his rifle. Dude was intense. We pressed on, killing everyone, all the wounded, all the retreaters we could see. Then, as dawn streaked the sky, the colonel finally called us back to camp.

I wasn't sure if I was more tired or hungry as I followed the rest of my team back on tired feet past the remains of smoking vehicles and sprawled bodies.

Jock caught me on the radio and I met him just inside the walls, along with the rest of our squad. We hadn't lost anyone, although Park had a cut on his forehead. We were muddy, battered, exhausted, but exhilarated to have driven off the attack. I had to admit, the Corwies were gutsy. If it hadn't been for the imperial air support, we might still be dodging mortars.

The colonel called the officers and sergeants to assemble inside the resort. Jock left us and we waited to see what would happen next. The minutes ticked on and our sweat cooled, the exhaustion really started to hit me but I wanted to know what was up before heading to sleep.

Eventually he came back, shaking his head. The Bastards gathered around him expectantly.

"Well, men, you aren't going to like this. But good news first. The colonel sends his congrats on successfully repelling last night's attack despite limited resources. He's real proud of you all. The other good news is that the second transport was not shot down. And now for the bad news. It pulled out and is headed back to Kantillon."

A murmur went up at this. Without our armor and artillery, this whole operation would be in jeopardy.

Jock continued, "To make a long story short, Wardogs will not be contracting with this particular supplier again. The transport company absolutely refused to make delivery due to the unexpected surface-to-air attacks on its first transport. The Kingdom of Corwistal has made it quite clear that they will attempt to shoot down any incoming ships from off-planet, and the shipping company presently in possession of our armor and artillery is not willing to take the risk of losing its transport. Of course, we will be seeking legal recourse on this point, and corporate has promised future drops to be arranged, yet for now, we must make do. Our techs hope to get drones up and going on something other than recon mode as well, which should help take some of the pressure off. Still, I have been assured that the cargo situation will be resolved as soon as possible, so don't go getting your panties in a bunch. For now, we are to clean our weapons, secure our gear, and we're going to arrange sleeping quarters and meals."

"As soon as possible," Park said, rubbing the bandage on his head. "Heard that before."

Yeah, for varying degrees of possible. I was pissed. We were all pissed. The last thing any of us wanted was to get killed by some hick on a backwater planet on behalf of a tin-pot emperor with delusions of grandeur, just because some chicken-hearted paper-pushers broke their contract with us.

Chapter 4

The Offensive

Sleeping quarters ended up being us packed like sardines into shipping containers, but I was too tired to care. We got five hours of blissful sleep, then were awakened by some horrid Ulimbese instrument which sounded like someone hammering on a howling drainpipe. The officers were already up and we dressed quickly, then were ushered into an open warehouse where Colonel Emerson stood in a crisp uniform beside an Ulimbese officer with a round and haughty face.

"Good afternoon, men," the colonel addressed us. "Excellent work repelling last night's attack and securing the armored division throttled in the valley. The Corwistalians put up considerably more resistance than expected, yet together we drove them back, which we could not have done as quickly without the air support of our Ulimbese allies, under the leadership of Stratarches Tark here."

The officer nodded his head slightly. "Stratarches" meant he was some kind of general. Guy looked young for a general.

"Intel told us to anticipate only minor resistance in the area," the colonel continued. "But yesterday we faced and turned back an entire division of Corwistalian regulars. Considering our success, we have agreed to launch a joint attack on Malliol, crushing the heart of the local opposition."

I remembered Malliol from the map I'd studied before we reached Ulixis. That was where the royal family resided for part of the year, a smaller city but quite rich. It was only a few kilometers out from here—

that way—I thought, orienting myself, then realized the armored column we'd gotten unstuck must have been on its way there. Yeah, that should cut down on the resistance.

"...and therefore, most of you we will be marching on foot. I have met with your officers and we are confident there will be a quick resolution to this crisis, especially as there are already two divisions of Ulimbese troops on their way. Take the city, you all collect cash and prizes, not to mention the good will of the Emperor and the Ulimbese people. Good luck to you all."

He saluted and we were dismissed to ready ourselves.

Well. We were walking. I smelled unfamiliar food and looked around for the source. "Grub's here, Tommy," Park said, pointing the way towards a series of large tents. Now that we had daylight, I could see the layout of the camp better than last night. It wasn't up to our military precision, but it was functional. Everything seemed makeshift and hurriedly thrown together, but they were hundreds of miles inside enemy lines. Marks saw us approaching and nodded. "Local food, boys. Line up and get it before it's gone."

I looked at the troughs of porridge, boiled roots, some greens and what appeared to be sausages in a white sauce. Looked decent. I bet we were paying for it, though, since we were supposed to be self-supplied. I hoped corporate was covering the extra food costs. Probably. I recognized one of the cooks and he waved to me. "Hope you like carbs, Tommy," he said cheerfully.

"Love 'em," I said, taking my place in line. "Ulimbese supply corps hooked us up," someone said. Probably looted the local stores, which would make sense. Dive in and take what you can before somebody else does.

I sat down to eat and a few minutes later a plump local woman came over with a cup of hot tea. She wasn't furry, and the only sign that she was Ulixian was her lightly golden skin.

"Thanks," I said as she smiled shyly at me.

"May I sit down?" she asked.

"Fine with me," I said, and she did.

"I just get tired of standing," she said. I nodded politely. Preaching to the choir, sister. I ignored her and took a sip of the tea. It wasn't bad. For tea, that is.

"I like the dog," she said, pointing at the Wardogs patch on my arm. I caught a glance from Cole at the next table, obviously trying to suppress a snicker at my expense. Our patch was awesome, though. Shaped like a shield, with a snarling pit bull lunging forward beneath a chain with a breaking link. "What's it say?" she asked.

I realized she couldn't read our text any better than I could read theirs.

"On the top there it reads, 'off the chain.'"

"That's nice," she said.

"Great," I said, swigging my tea and standing up. "Hey, thanks for the tea, lady. Take care of yourself."

I walked away and dumped my dishes, ignoring the snickers of a couple of the guys. "Chubby chaser," Cole snickered as I passed.

"Just like your daddy," I said, waving him off.

Two hours later our march began, just as the sun was setting. We had a squad out front and a squad in back as advance and rear guards, plus a squad to the left and on the right of the company as flanking support. I was in the right guard. This time we stuck to the road, making our way through the ups and downs of the countryside until we reached the point where the armored column had bogged down the previous night. Multiple wrecked vehicles still sat there, some smoking, but the Ulimbese and our boys had done well moving out that which could be moved.

It was a long night but uneventful. The Corwistalians who lived had retreated. Some of our Ulimbese allies passed us in trucks and more armored vehicles, though others were also on the march. A few of their gunships flew over, probably the same ones that had broken the tide last night.

At around midnight we moved off the road to allow through some heavy transports. As they passed I saw some huge howitzers that looked pretty similar to those our drones had taken out the night before. One after the other passed us, towed behind big-engined trucks. "That'll soften 'em up," Rocky laughed from my left.

We experienced the first resistance within sight of the city. We couldn't see much of anything thanks to the ridges and trees, then we hit a ridge and looked down into a valley and there it was—Malliol, lit up like a casino, with searchlights playing out across the fields leading up to the city.

Some fairytale castle spires rose like crystals above the city as we started down into the valley. Now we were in the fields, mostly stubble at this time of year except for winter grains. The air was misty and chill and I heard the lowing of cattle somewhere in the night. Rows of leafless grape vines twisted on wires and I spied a row of wind turbines here and there above the fields, still in the calm night air. Now and again we passed a farm house but most of them had their lights off. I assumed the families had fled. The night was quiet and cool.

CRACK! there was a shot and one of our men fell. Off the road—to the right—an earth bank. "Sniper!" someone yelled. "We got him," Jock yelled in the radio. "Keep us covered." He slapped my shoulder and we took off. On my thermals I could just make out two signatures, about 100 meters up behind a wall. Jock and I ran at a diagonal and jumped the wall, then nailed them as they tried to flee.

When we got back to the line our men had already moved the wounded soldier and we were back on our way.

That was the last bit of trouble until we hit the base near the outskirts of the city. The big guns were already in place, and the armor was arranged in a bristling metal wall pointed towards Malliol.

Almost as we arrived, the Ulimbese cannon boomed with an opening volley into the city. From behind the large cannon and from scattered locations on high ground, mortar teams sent in shells, streaking up and above and then down into the fairytale city.

The lights in Malliol started to go out in patches as the heavy projectiles did their work. And the Ulimbese had plenty of ammo on hand. There was not much return fire coming out of the city. The Corwies had some artillery of their own, but their counterfire was ineffective. They must not have boresighted the surrounding heights, which suggested that their commanders were both ill-prepared and incompetent.

Colonel Emerson informed us that the first offensive would begin right after the shelling and would be conducted by three regiments of crack imperial troops. Their flashy uniforms cracked me up as we watched them move into position. Someone should have told them that war isn't a fashion shoot.

The guns pounded and pounded, bombarding the city for an hour, turning it into a hellscape, now lit by flames more than electric lights, while beneath the covering fire, the Ulimbese infantry advanced behind the armored columns.

And then the guns ceased. The Ulimbese must be entering the outskirts. And then, from behind us, we heard the gunships take to the air, then fly over. They had multiple guns on their bottoms which could cut down troops from above like a scythe through wheat.

"Give these guys another eye in the sky," Colonel Emerson said over the radio. "Get a drone up there."

The armor started trading fire with pockets of resistance.

I found a good vantage point, zoomed my goggles and tuned in to the chatter on the Ulimbese channel.

"...main road—we have barricades here..."

"...snipers—upper floors—neutralize..."

"...machine gun nests, multiple...we have incoming..."

"...take cover...watch it...three o'clock..."

"...gonna need more air cover here—bring 'em in—a lot of incoming!"

I saw plenty of fire coming out along the roads, blinking, tracers coming down from above, and then the Ulimbese gunships swept in, launching missiles towards the fortified Corwistalian strongpoints. They took out a few in spectacular fashion. I hoped the gunships had armor as they flew low over the city walls, sweeping the ground with fire. I didn't see much in the way of return fire, as they went deeper into the city, seeking out targets. And then I heard the Ulimbese radio erupt into panicked chatter, then saw the flash of a gunship hitting the ground and disappearing into a ball of fire. I zoomed out, then saw a streak of light lance upwards from inside the city and take down a second gunship.

"...surface-to-air! We have spotted multiple SAM teams! Repeat, pull back the gunships! Surface-to-air!"

But the order came too late and the gunships were in too deep. A swarm of missiles streaked skywards from all sides and enough of them found their targets. In a matter of minutes, the Ulimbese had lost their air support, and then the machine guns opened up again, keeping the Ulimbese troops on their bellies behind the advancing armor. Then there was another fireball as an anti-tank gun took out one of the Ulimbese tanks. Despite the city being softened by artillery, the imperials were getting chewed to pieces by the tough Corwistalian defenders.

"...unable to take out defense, secondary road, concrete slabs..."

"...on the East, still encountering heavy fire, unable to advance..."

And then I saw Marks slam his fist into his palm. He'd heard something on our channel. I switched back.

"...gone blank, we lost it."

"We can't afford to launch another. There's no way to get new ones right now."

"Roger—out."

We'd lost another drone then. I wondered how many we had left. Rocky nudged me out of my observation. "We need to get in there, Tommy, show 'em how to do it." I'm sure the brass were thinking the same thing. And if I knew what they had in mind, we were gonna get called in to play tag. Laser tag.

A few moments of fruitless skirmishing later, the Ulimbese retreated as their big guns opened up again, suppressing the enemy in order to give them a chance to pull back without being pursued. It wasn't a rout, but it was a sound ass-kicking. Once the defeated, demoralized Ulimbese had regained the safety of the camp, Colonel Emerson called the brass together, then a few minutes later Marks told us the deal.

"Here's the situation, boys. We're facing not only the city militia, we're up against two regiments of regulars and a company of the prince's elite guard. We are going to hit them again with a 10-minute bombardment, then you will go in well-supplied with smoke, tag points of resistance, in particular machine gun and missile batteries, then we will take them out with missile-bearing drones. We lost one drone playing spy over the city, so no more of that. Instead, you will tag, we will get the drones in, hit the targets, and get them out. The colonel doesn't want to lose any more eyes in the sky, especially as we have no idea when we will be re-supplied. We strike at dawn."

The sky was already a pale grey on the horizon, and the fields were thick with mist. It was almost time—and that mist would help us, as would the still air.

"Hey Tommy—why do they think it's better to lose men than drones?" Ward asked me. I turned to him in surprise, not knowing he was beside me.

"We cost less," I said. "Also, if you lose your eyes in the sky, you run the risk of losing a lot more men. We're probably going to lose a few men when we go in, but if we lose our ability to take out their hard points and see what's in front of us, we're going to lose a helluva lot more. But don't worry, the colonel seems to know what he's doing. And even if corporate didn't give a rat's ass for our lives, they would care about losing money. Each man down is an insurance payout, plus they have to hire a replacement who probably requires additional training. They don't want that! Make sense?"

He nodded, apparently satisfied. We all have to learn as we go along, I guess.

The cannons pounded over our heads as we launched smoke into the field and went low, scrabbling from cover to cover. We followed the edge of a stone wall for a time, then jumped into a thicket.

Park whispered a curse as he yanked a thorn out of his hand. We could see the roadblocks and enemy troops ahead despite the smoke. Our goggles were switched to discriminate. I thanked the war gods that they snuck in just below Ulixis' tech level.

The guns behind us ceased as we were now too close to the enemy defenses. The thicket ended in the remnants of a corn field, corrugated by cultivation and currently thick with the rustling stubble of dry and felled stalks. Across the field I could see lots of our squads crawling foot by foot, covered by the repeated launch of new smoke grenades. *RAT-TA-TAT-TAT!* The chatter of enemy machine guns tore over the field and right over my head. I was bound and determined not to take another hit. Right now we were a ways out, so staying low was the best bet.

Puffs of dirt flew up here and there as enemy rounds sought blindly for targets, then we hit a sprawling vineyard. Jock waved us in and we followed the rows of grapes, knowing even without smoke the Corwistalian gunners wouldn't see us. Unlike the Ulimbese armor, we could hide.

We got on our feet now, crouching to stay below the 1.5 meter height of the vines, going single file behind Jock, who was guiding us inwards by map, as we couldn't see the machine gun nests thanks to the roll of the hill and the vines. Every little bit, we'd crawl under a few rows, then go along a row again. Multiple other squads were also taking advantage of the vines. It also saved our limited supply of smoke grenades.

Then we came to a large barn at the end of the vineyard. Jock opened the back of the barn—it was unlocked—and we went through. Inside sat a tractor, keys in the ignition. Tools, jars, racks of dry corn, even a chainsaw, all there in an unlocked barn. Trusting people, these

Corwistalians—or perhaps the owners had fled for their lives and left their material goods. Yeah, probably the latter.

We looked out the entrance of the barn. Through the smoke we could see another cornfield and a simple white house with bushes, beyond which was the road again. As an experiment I pulled down my goggles and could barely see 20 meters ahead. "Good," I muttered. "Can't see anything?" Park said. "Yeah, clear as mud."

"Let's hope the Corwies don't have optics like ours," he said.

"They don't," Jock replied. "We've got the advantage, so long as the wind doesn't rise."

And then we were off again, crawling low across the field. Enemy fire chattered here and there but it was distant—until the slope changed and we were suddenly looking down at the outer edges of the enemy's defenses.

"Squad—recon—let's get our bearings."

We peered down towards Malliol, seeing the city for the first time. It wasn't a great view, thanks to all the smoke. I'm sure on an average morning the spires glittered in the red of the rising sun like an elven citadel amidst the rolling fields and all that shit, but right now it was a stark green and black image in my goggles.

They had blocked off the road with piles of junk—everything from vehicles to massive concrete block, sandbags, and coils of razor wire. We could see more than one road into the city from our slight elevation, and they were all a complete obstacle course.

I knew the colonel was receiving film feeds from some of our goggle recorders. Though he almost certainly wasn't watching them himself, the techs would feed him data from streams of interest.

Our guys were all over the place now—I could see them scattered here and there, crawling under the smoke. I zoomed in on the enemy positions, looking to see what we faced. Beyond the scattered pockets of artillery, cannons and mortars were plenty of troops. I tried to make sense of the various groups based on the data feeds I'd absorbed on the trip into the system. Some of those guys were Corwistalian regulars. Uniforms were what we'd already seen in previous assaults. Then there were guys in simple slacks, shirts, books and caps—more like police. Those must be city militia, local volunteers. And then—yes, I saw some seriously decked out guys in armor, with crested helmets. Those were elite troops of some sort. Maybe the prince's guard, actually.

Colonel Emerson's voice came over the radio, calm and clear. "Men, move in close. Bravo and Lima company—send your squads to take the Palace Drive entrance. Delta, move around to Fairview—and get those troops on the bridge. Kilo—continue on your present course down towards the main road and bust 'em up. Squads—get me tags on everything we need to hit as you go and we'll drone 'em for you. You must break the artillery on the edges of the city—they can't hit us effectively from inside. Take 'em down!"

"Launch smoke, Kilo!" came the voice of Captain Marks, and our guys did, as did others. Four-eyes had a launcher. Jock was sticking to his tablet and just his rifle, navigating us in. I had a few hand-thrown smoke grenades and a few primitive frags but from this far out they weren't worth anything.

Sporadic enemy fire answered the smoke but the Corwistalians obviously didn't know where to shoot. We ducked and ran in quickly, staying behind what cover we could as we came into a more suburban area. Houses, kids' play equipment, parked cars—we were running down sidewalks through the smoke, getting close to the nests. Here and there along the road we saw abandoned belongings and trash, marking a quick evacuation of the civilians. There was a lot of smoke in the air thanks to multiple burning houses and vehicles from the shelling. We were separated from the rest of Kilo company now as teams spread out through the neighborhood. It was just the eight of us. Just how I liked it. Quick and deadly.

A rattle of fire tore past me, shredding the leaves off an oak and I ducked lower. That was close—just up ahead somewhere.

"There," Jock hissed. We jumped a hedge, then saw a chainlink fence on the other side of a small road with neat sidewalks. Past the fence—there! The barrel of a machine gun lit up from the hillside rising above a field—a sports field. I eyed it up—yeah, they were plenty high enough to spray rounds down to the main road. Sandbags surrounded the position, and I could make out at least a half dozen men manning the nest.

"Drone team—I have a target," Jock said. "Bring the fire—on the tag." As he said it, Park popped up his tripod and lit the targeting laser, putting a drone-visible dot right inside the nest. Fortunately we were using an invisible spectrum laser—if we'd been one tech level down, that thing would have glittered in the smoke and brought fire on our heads quicker than you can say shock and awe.

"Now we wait," Jock said—but even as he did, a vehicle rolled slowly up the street between us and the park, coming through the neighborhood. It was a truck, two guys in the back, two in the cab. "Back behind the hedge, keep that laser on target," Jock ordered.

"Going real slow, Sarge," Private Leighton observed. Rocky already had taken aim with his rifle.

"Smoke—they can't see well. And hold fire," Jock said. "Not our target. Just stay down."

They rolled closer, then closer. And then they stopped at our end of the block—right in the path of the targeting laser.

Jock cursed. "Turn it off—Park—off! If that drone is over us right now–" Park grabbed for the tripod but snagged his uniform on the hedge, knocking it to the ground with a clatter.

Then everything happened all at once. The guys in the back of the truck ducked and opened fire—Rocky fired right back at them—and then the radio erupted into static and clods of dirt flew into my face as I staggered back from the fence to find a better position.

"Abort!" Jock yelled into the radio. "Abort the drone now!" But they didn't hear us. All there was on the other end was noise. We were being jammed.

More gunfire! I tripped over a kid's bicycle and sprawled to the ground, ducking behind the step-up porch of the house as a spray of bullets sent chunks of brick spattering around me. I heard a scream of pain as my team sent back answering fire and saw the driver of the truck slumped against the wheel. I looked up but saw nothing. If that drone were overhead right now!

One of the men in the back of the truck was down and the two others had taken cover behind it, blindly popping off rounds towards our position. Behind a tree Jock sent answering fire. I ran around behind the house to get behind the truck. I came around the side and stayed low, spying Rocky, who was already there, crouching and aiming from behind a brick planter. He took out the soldier behind the back tire with a burst of fire, then suddenly threw his arms up, jerking like a puppet as a spray of fire came from somewhere else. Dammit! I hit the ground hard. Where the hell did that come from?

I scanned the area in front of me, then saw two soldiers across the road in the field, crouching down low. One of them had shot Rocky, probably seeing his muzzle flash through the smoke. I snapped a smoke grenade off my belt and threw it into the road. It bounced and hit the chainlink, bringing another rattle of fire.

"Get that laser," Jock shouted. "Get the laser on target right now! I'm pinned down here!"

More gunfire rattled from the road in front of the house.

The smoke was thick now and I crawled on my belly to where Park had propped the tripod. Along the way I ran into the crumpled form of Jones. His helmet was on the ground beside him. I couldn't tell if he was dead or what. There was no time to check him out and we'd all be crispy critters if that laser wasn't realigned fast.

"Get me smoke!" I yelled into the radio, and a second later a smoke bomb flew overhead, hiding me in a thick, choking grey cloud.

There were bullets whizzing past as our guys traded fire with the Corwies but I don't think I heard anything. The blood pulsed in my head, my focus narrowed to a tunnel, and I thought of nothing but that laser! I even thought I could hear the buzz of an approaching drone. I finally reached the tripod and dragged it fifteen feet, then pulled it up and pointed it toward the gun emplacement above the field. I made sure it was as on-target as I could place it, then dropped to the ground just as the searing hiss of an incoming missile tore through the sky above. The flash was blinding in my goggles and the blast that followed was deafening—tango down!

Or was it? As the smoke and dust cleared, I saw the missile strike had struck the front of the pit, rather than inside it. It was possible that there might even be someone alive behind the sandbags, or that the gun itself might be operational if the Corwies managed to reman it. But if anyone was still alive in there, they'd be out of it, bleeding out of their ears and concussed into walking vegetables.

"Aces, Tommy!" came Jock's voice over the radio, thick with relief. "Well done, Falkland. That was too close!"

The distraction of the missile strike must have given our boys the advantage because I no longer heard any gunfire. I looked around and saw three of our guys in the road by the truck, standing over a fallen Corwie. I remembered Jones and went back to him. His eyes were open now and he was staring up at the sky, blinking heavily.

"Hey Jones," I said. "You still with us?"

He turned his head and focused on me, then gave a slight nod, then winced. "Got...hit..."

I picked up his helmet. The front was dented.

"Shot..." he said, trying to get up.

"No," I said. "If a bullet had hit your helmet there you'd be dead." I looked in front of him, where some blocks lined a little garden path, then found one which had been smashed to bits. "Must have been a chunk of rock, Corporal."

He brought himself up unsteadily on his elbows. His forehead had an angry red slash mark from his helmet being struck. He was going to need medical attention. I helped him sit up and get his back against a small tree just as the rest of the team joined us.

"He alright?" Jock said to me. I shook my head. "Probably concussed. Lucky, though." I tossed him the helmet. "We're gonna have to help him."

"Yeah," said Jock. "Where's Rocky?"

"They got him. He's back there in the road."

Jock cursed. "Go check on him, Four-eyes. Park, grab that target laser." He stood and looked over at the nest we'd hit. I followed his gaze and we had the same thought at the same time. "That gun still looks operational," he said. "We're gonna have to go spike it ourselves."

"What happened to our drone channel?" I said. "Jammed?"

"That's my guess," Jock said as Four-eyes returned. "He's dead?" Jock said, seeing the expression on Corporal Raymond's face. Four-eyes nodded. "Crazy bastard," Jock said. "One of the best. Okay, Raymond, you and Park get him out of the road and leave him by the house. They'll come get him." We all had tags linked to our vital signs. Vitals cease, tag emits a signal. Easier than combing battlefields looking for corpses.

"Ward, help Jones—we'll take that gun in person."

Jock radioed for backup and found another squad was near enough to assist in taking the cannon. As he directed them in, we found an entrance through the fence. Our backup was about six blocks away but we still didn't see any troops near the nest, so we started across the field without them, keeping low. The wind was picking up and the smoke started to clear, though as we crossed the field we came into view of the spires of the urban center and saw it wreathed in rising smoke. I wanted more here—I felt naked. The clatter of far-off guns and the occasional impact of a missile told me our other teams were staying busy. The radios for each squad were trackable back at base, allowing for us to find each other quickly. Once Jock called for backup, we would be found relatively simply just by keying in his signal and tracking it via field tablet.

We hit the edge of the field and then the terrain turned up sharply in a scrubby ridge of eroded red clay and rock. Anemic thorn bushes and wildflowers hung on to the rough slope in patches and we clutched at what we could to make the ascent. Above us was the ring of sandbags and as I got closer, I saw one side of it was thrown everywhere and scattered in a big mess. At about half-way up I heard a shout and looked down behind me, thinking our backup had arrived. With a shock I realized two jeeps carrying a squad of royal guard were racing towards us across the field.

"Faster!" I yelled. "Get to the gun nest!" As I said it they opened fire from below, but we were almost there…almost there!

And then we were over the wall of sand bags, Ward almost throwing Jones over in his haste—and another crack of fire came from beyond the royal guard. There was our backup—but they were in the field, without cover. The Royal Guard were behind their jeeps and sniping at our boys. I looked around to see four dead men inside the ring of sandbags, half buried in sand and torn up by the blast, except for one almost broken in half over the seat of the cannon. Jock, Park, Four-eyes and Leighton were trying to snipe the guards from over the bags but they were firing back, so the boys had to keep their heads down. Then I looked at the barrel of the machine gun, which seemed intact, shoved the body off the seat, swung the barrel around, said a prayer to Ares, and fired!

I came up too high at first but walked the barrel down, destroying the jeeps and cutting the enemy troops to pieces.

The look on Jock's face was priceless. All of them had jumped and ducked when I pulled the trigger, focused completely on the enemy below.

"Thanks, boys!" came a voice over the radio. "We lost one down here, second wounded. Those guys would have had us all in another moment."

"Thank Corporal Falkland," Jock radioed back, then turned to me. "Okay, Tommy. Nice one. But that gun could have blown to pieces…not exactly the smartest approach."

"Yes sir. You are correct," I replied seriously. "I am stupid, sir."

His face cracked into a grin. "Naw, it was awesome." He slapped me on the back. In a moment, we were joined by the men from the second squad, one of whom had to be helped up as his arm hung limp and bloody at his side.

I looked down from the nest. It had a great view, sweeping over the neighborhood and covering the road. If it hadn't been for drones, we would have had a hard time hitting it. I looked over the edge of the sandbags on the right side and spotted two more bodies, thrown partially down the ridge.

The position was excellent, and since the gun was working…"Jock," I said. "Tell me—why shouldn't we hold this gun for now?"

"Objective was to destroy them," he said, "but it is tempting. We could take potshots at enemy troops for a solid 180 degrees." He looked up. Above us the rock rose into almost a sheer cliff face. "Yeah, tempting," he said. "Though they could probably take it back if they came by with some bigger truck-mounted artillery. We might be the sitting ducks, then. Probably better to blow it and go hit the next one."

"I could stay," said the Wardog with the busted arm. One of his teammates had tied it up already.

"Can you man this gun with one arm, Private Walters?" the other squad leader asked him. The injured man grinned.

"Are Achernarni chicks blue?" he said.

No one knew, but it was obvious the guy had guts. He sat up behind the gun, swung it back and forth experimentally and nodded. "No problem, Lieutenant Fick. I'll stay."

"I'm with him," Jones said. "I've got a helluva a headache but I think I can still spot."

"Anyone else volunteer to stay?" Fick asked the rest of us. No one said yes. Tired as we were, staying behind and waiting wasn't in our blood.

Fick shrugged. "That's what I figured. Corporal Goodman, you stay with Walters and Jones. You be his backup eyes. And here," he said, taking an explosive charge from his pack. "Blow it up when we get called in. If all goes well, someone will pick you up again when the main body rolls into the city this evening."

Goodman nodded, then we grabbed our packs and headed out in search of another nest to tag. After some triangulation with home base, we found another one two miles on, tucked up on a hill beneath a water tower.

Park got the targeting laser perfect on that one. If you never heard the sound of a drone strike causing a massive water tower to explode and fall on a machine gun nest, well, you just haven't lived. It was beautiful.

But not as beautiful as the news we got that evening as we watched sun sink into the faraway ocean. We'd pulled it off and the Ulimbese armor and the rest of our boys were moving in. The city was ours, with the exception of the royal palace itself.

Booyah.

Chapter 5

The Surrender

The royal palace had been left almost unscathed by the shelling and skirmishes of the last day. Located deep inside the city in an island of green, its walled design hinted at a feudal past. Or maybe just an eccentric king. We'd eaten on the run, taken stimulants, and connected with the advancing troops as they came up the main road, ready for whatever happened. When we reached the palace, things came to a halt. Now I sat on the edge of a fountain with the rest of my squad. Behind me, a naked dame was spitting water out of her mouth. Not a real naked dame, mind you—she was made of marble. Good thing, too, because she was ejecting about five gallons a minute. The beauty of the landscaping around us was a weird contrast with the tension in the air and the two opposing forces facing each other across a sea of expensive paving stones, sculptures, banks of flowers and whatever you call bushes carved into circles and squares.

We'd actually caught a few hours sleep on the grass the previous night. Our brass were talking with the enemy brass and now we were killing time until whatever happened next.

"Probably going to send us in to take the place," I said.

"You think?" Leighton asked, gesturing towards the palace. "Those guys up there behind the barricades are the prince's royal guard. The best they've got."

"Maybe," I said. "But last time I checked, we're better than that." Despite my confidence in our superiority, though, I wasn't about to sign on for an all-out assault on the palace. Bum-rushing them through the gardens when they had walls and barricades and machine guns, no way. We weren't going to find any cover behind the topiary, that's for sure.

"Yeah, well, I wouldn't want to do a direct assault even if they were ranked thirty-fifth in the subsector," Leighton said. "They're dug in too good for us to go in light. If they're half-way decent, we'd lose half our guys trying to take it. Better if they pound them with the big guns."

"Sure," said Jock from where he sat beneath a tree with a perfectly braided triple trunk. "I doubt the colonel would make us go straight in, anyhow. They probably don't want to wreck the place if they're intending to keep it. If we went at night with enough smoke, we could probably go through the gazebos in the rose garden over on the side and set some charges on the wall, then get inside."

"Maybe they've mined the rose garden," Park mused, chewing on a protein bar.

"I doubt it," Leighton said. "That collection of roses is highly valuable." He actually sounded serious.

I laughed. "Don't be a faggot. What do you know about flowers?"

He grinned sheepishly. "Hey, I like flowers. My Grandma grew roses."

"Geez, Leighton. Maybe your Grandma should have joined War-dogs," Jock said, his voice dripping with sarcasm. "Sounds like she'd have some great intel for us."

"I dunno, couldn't be much worse than the other intel we've had lately," I pointed out.

"Think the king is inside?" Park said, crumbling up the wrapper of his protein bar and throwing it into the fountain.

"Nope," said Jock. "But the crown prince is. And pick up your trash."

Park shrugged and fished out the brown wrapper.

And then we heard a whistling sound, followed by the deep crump of a single round striking the city.

"Spotter round," Jock said as we watched the thin column of smoke rise up from where the shell landed. "Huh. That means an FFE is incoming. They are going to just smash the place up."

We hurried back behind our lines. Jock gestured and pointed back behind us at some hulking gray artillery pieces. During the night the Ulimbese had brought a pair of massive 120mm howitzers and placed them up on the hills with us to permit direct fire. They had aimed both of them to take a bead on the castle now, even as and more spotting rounds from the supporting artillery landed. The prince's guard wasn't going to have a chance, no matter how good they were. That much firepower would smash them to pieces.

And then it started. Mortars flew, cannons fired, and heavy machine guns opened up, pinning down the prince's guard whenever they dared to show their faces. They were surrounded and overmatched. One of the towers on the edge of the castle collapsed into rubble. Bricks and marble splintered and cracked, and gargoyles and standards fell from the battlements amidst breaking glass and the deafening roar of the guns.

And then—after less than ten minutes of hellish bombardment—a white banner rose from the top wall of the castle—the intergalactic symbol of surrender!

The big guns ceased almost instantly, and except for a secondary explosion or two, the field of battle fell silent. Smoke rose from the pockmarked palace and the prince's guard began to appear on the battlements, holding their hands high. And yet, as I reviewed the scene with my old-fashioned optical binocs, I saw the marble lady was intact and still spitting, just as if nothing had happened.

Jock looked at me and I looked back and shrugged. Looked like we got off easy this time.

For a few minutes we stood, and smoked, and made small talk waiting for our next orders, until Captain Marks walked over and nodded to us. "Sergeant Hanley, men. I have a new assignment for you."

"Yes sir," Jock responded.

"Crown Prince Etna-Harald has surrendered," Marks announced. "You and your men will be part of a 16-man platoon assembled to escort Colonel Emerson and Stratarches Tark as they take the prince into custody. You will command the platoon, Sergeant. Pick your men and meet Colonel Emerson at the command tent in thirty minutes."

As Marks left, Jock turned to us. "So men, feel like rubbing shoulders with royalty?"

Park shrugged. "Do we get better food?"

"You can buy your own with the money we're making. All right, all of you guys are with me, and I'll pick some hardcases from Kilo Company. Where's Four-eyes?"

"He was hanging around the Ulimbese com guys earlier," Park said.

"Probably fighting AI withdrawal," I said.

"Yeah, probably," Jock said. "We'll take him if we can find him too. You guys cleaned up as best as you can."

I looked down at my stained uniform and mud-encrusted boots. I'd put my rifle to rights, but that was the only thing I'd been able to clean.

Jock must have been thinking the same thing, because he frowned as he looked us over. "Yeah, on second thought, let's see if we can requisition something a little better for our brush with the blue bloods."

Less than a half-hour later, dressed in clean clothes and armor Jock had found somewhere, we were lined up in two rows around Stratarches Tark and Colonel Emerson, walking down a fancy-looking path towards the wall around the castle. It was open and manned by Ulimbese guards. We walked through and I saw rows of bodies stacked against the inside of the wall, along with disarmed Ulimbese soldiers and prince's guard lined up along the wall of the castle itself. A few soldiers were walking down the row and photographing each face as they went, logging them into the computer for ID. Both living and dead would be treated the same way.

About forty feet in front of the castle entrance, Colonel Emerson called us to a halt. We waited, at attention, for about a minute—and then the door opened and the prince stepped out. He wore black pants and a lavender silk shirt with white ruffs, and a red cape. On his head was a simple circlet of silver, over short brown hair. Except for the clothes, he looked pretty ordinary to me. Ordinary and exhausted.

Behind the prince were six men in sharp sky-blue uniforms and white gloves. His honor guard, carrying ancient one-shot rifles. I guessed they were unloaded, not like they'd be able to do much if they tried. Stratarches Tark nodded slightly to the prince and he and his guards walked out to meet us, stiff and silent. We fell in around them, but instead of walking back the way we'd come, we went around a sweeping walk behind the castle to a parking garage, now manned by Ulimbese soldiers.

There we waited as four vehicles were brought around. They were nondescript, armored types that might have carried spooks for any service. If I'm not mistaken, the prince had a bit of surprise on his face. I don't think he expected this.

Stratarches Tark then addressed the prince. "Your Highness, the emperor has empowered me to speak on his behalf. With the imperial power vested in me, and in appreciation of your surrender of your person without further resistance or bloodshed, we are granting you parole, provided you travel directly to the royal capitol."

"What of my men?" the prince said, turning for the first time to look the stratarches in the face.

Stratarches Tark nodded slightly. "Of your Royal Guard, perhaps 200 remain. They will be taken into imperial custody, where they will be treated with respect and honor. The city militia and the regulars soldiers being disarmed, and they, too, will be paroled after they are processed and their identities are recorded."

The prince's mouth was a thin line as he took the news in silence. Then he nodded slightly.

"I accept your conditions." He paused for a moment, then nodded firmly. "And I thank you for your magnanimity in victory, Stratarches."

"Take your vehicles, Prince Etna-Harald," Tark said, after returning the prince's nod with a formal bow. "Please travel directly to the capitol with no deviations. Your vehicles are fully fueled and we have cleared the highway to the north. You will not be molested."

Diplomatic matters being settled, the Corwistalian prince and his escort got into the idling cars and slowly left us behind.

And that was that.

Or so I thought.

Chapter 6

One Down, Two to Go

Four hours later I found myself on a clunky unmarked VTOL aircraft along with the rest of the platoon, heading to parts unknown. The pilot and copilot were in civilian clothes, as were the two guys in cargo. One of them looked familiar but I couldn't place him. You see a lotta stiffs in this business.

The sun was setting as I looked down over the countryside. We'd been told we had a special bonus contract, but I had no idea what it was. We'd been given new rifles, heavier weapons shooting larger, armor-piecing rounds, then marched up the ramp into this shuddering deathtrap of a low-tech flying machine.

For most of us, it was more terrifying than actual combat.

After seeing no explanations were forthcoming, I leaned my head back and shut my eyes, exhaustion overcoming my curiosity.

I awakened to Park shaking my shoulder. We were landing. There was a rough bump, then a settling of struts, then the crew popped the doors. I unstrapped, jumped up, and followed the platoon out into the darkness. I pulled on my goggles and looked around. We were in a stretch of tall rolling grass near a highway. Judging by the thermal signatures, we were probably the only people for miles, though I couldn't see over all the hills. Not even an all-night diner, just empty grassland.

When we were all out and some cargo had been dumped by the crew, the helo took off and left us. In the middle of nowhere.

All eyes were now on Jock.

The sergeant cleared his throat and addressed us. "As you all know by now, you're on a special mission of utmost importance. We're out here to—"

"Kill the prince," a Wardog whistled. "That crazy Ulimbese general sent us here to kill the prince."

"Shut up, Cole," Jock said.

"Yessir," the man said.

"Bad manners aside, though," Jock paused, "that is our objective."

There were murmurs around the group. We were mercs. It wasn't like we wouldn't shank an enemy in the dark. The emperor must've felt the same way and we were the shank. But this was stone cold.

"You will of course receive bonuses," Jock said. "Now, we've seen the prince and his men. We've also seen their vehicles. That's why were here. Right now their convoy is being tracked by drone." He paused and took out his tablet. "Based on their progress thus far, they'll be here within the hour."

"We're going to set up an ambush in the road here," he pointed to a bend in the road, "but as of right now, there is a civilian vehicle on the road roughly 10 minutes ahead of him so we'll wait for that to pass, then we'll create an L-shaped ambush just past that bend, with a machine gun team in the road with 10 more of our guys in a row along the creek bed. They enter the kill zone and the machine gun opens up, then the long leg of the L takes them out."

"Sir, no RPGs?" asked Goodman.

Jock shook his head. "No RPGs this time. Our client requires a decent photo of the deceased, not a splatter painting. Now, I want a fire team a quarter kilometer before the L, right where the hill peaks, in case they manage to turn around or get nervous. This team will also act as our spotters.

"A quarter kilometer beyond the L, I want another machine gun team, just in case they follow SOP and mash the gas and somehow get through our first ambush. We'll have eight men in the grass keeping rifles along the long leg of the L. You have likely already noted the rifle upgrades, as well as the armor-piercing rounds. No one gets out alive."

"Understood," we said, then found our positions.

I was between Private Goodman and Four-eyes. "Hey Falkland," Goodman said to me. "How come we don't just have some guys in the road pretending to be a road crew? Hard-hats and a barricade and all that. Maybe a flare. We could get them to slow down, then pow!"

"I dunno," I said.

"Well I know," Four-eyes said. "You do that and they'll know something is up. Guys that do security for important people would smell that old trick a kilometer away. A group of military-age guys hanging around a barrier in the middle of nowhere in the middle of the night? Might as well put up a billboard that says 'free assassinations ahead.'"

"Oh. That makes sense," Goodman nodded. "I never got to do this kind of cloak and dagger stuff before."

"Stick around," I said. "We also do windows."

About forty minutes later, lights appeared over the hill about a quarter mile distant and we ducked low in the tall grass. I watched as the lights got closer. It was a big shipping centipede, hauling multiple containers behind it. Then it passed into the night, its taillights melting off into the faraway darkness. Jock's voice crackled. "Fire teams—set up now. That was the only civvie. Remaining men, hold your positions and prepare to engage."

Seconds ticked by as I crouched in the grass. Sweat dripped inside my goggles and I checked the safety on my rifle for the second time. I was tense. We'll pull it off fine—stay cool Tommy, I told myself.

"We have visual," came the voice of Park from the top of the hill. I was next to Four-eyes. He was perfectly calm, waiting with the tip of his tongue sticking out the side of his mouth as he looked down his sight and waited for our targets to approach. Five long minutes ticked by, then I saw the light glowing at the top of the hill, followed by a set of headlights, then three more. Definitely the prince's caravan. They took the corner and we opened up on them.

We fired from multiple locations along the road, the armor-piercing rounds slamming into and through the unmarked vehicles, penetrating both their armor and their reinforced glass. All four vehicles were armored, but the bullet-proofing wasn't designed to stand up to that amount of heavy gunfire.

Two of the vehicles crashed almost immediately, their drivers having been shot dead in the initial barrage. The third slewed around and came to a near-stop, and one hard case in the back seat somehow managed to open a rear door and shoot back at us before he caught an AP round in the chest. The last vehicle actually did a 180 and tried to beat hasty retreat before it too drifted off to the side of the road and came to a dead halt on the left embankment.

"Cease fire!" came the call. There was no movement except for the dripping of fluids and the steam and smoke rising from the vehicles' engines. The cars looked like they'd driven through Hell's own hail, with all the windows shattered and the doors filled with dozens of round holes.

"Move in," Jock said. "Stay alert."

I was one of the closest guys so I got there first. I held my Katzer up as I peered into the middle vehicle. I put it down once I looked inside. The four occupants were definitely KIA. They'd never had a chance. The same report came from the other cars. We'd killed them all.

The second car contained the target. We opened the door and pulled the prince's body out onto the road so Four-eyes could take pics. His clothes were soaked with blood and it took us a little while to find his crown in the car, but Jock insisted so we could put it on his head for the photo. The guy had taken a round in the neck, another took off the side of his skull, a few more in the torso but you could still recognize him. More or less.

"Jackpot," Jock said coldly. "All right, Four-eyes, take some tissue samples so we can evidence the kill and we'll get out of here.

Then he frowned and held up one hand, putting the other to his earpiece. "Captain? Yeah, we're good and the tango is down. Yes, copy that, thank you." He turned back to us. "Captain says bravo zulu, everyone. He also says the highway to the north of us is already being barricaded by Kingdom forces, but we'll go off-road and bypass them." Jock looked down at the body of the man we'd just assassinated. "Goodnight, sweet prince."

I was happy just adding up the bonus we'd nailed down, but then Four-eyes had to ruin it with one of his untimely remarks.

"Man," he said, eyeing one of the sample tubes he was stowing away. "I have to think the Corwies are going to be some kind of pissed!"

Chapter 7

Midnight Raid

The flight back to base was silent. We touched down, cleaned up and hit the sack. I was asleep as soon as my head hit my pack. A few hours later I awakened, wondering where I was. I looked up at rough wood beams over my head and smelled hay. *Why the devil does my back hurt?* was my first thought, followed by remembering I got hit in the back. Then I remembered I had just assassinated a prince the night before. How about that! Then I looked around and remembered I was in a big old barn turned mercenary barracks.

Okay, Tommy, now you're all up to date. What now?

That hit last night seemed like a stupid thing for the Ulimbese to order, especially since they were holding so much Corwistalian territory. Showing mercy would have made so much more sense. There were witnesses to the prince's surrender. Whacking him like that just made the Emperor look like a turncoat jackass.

I wondered if the King of Corwistal knew about it yet. Then a dark thought struck me. What if the Ulimbese didn't know about it either? What if it was us?

"Hey, Tommy, things just got interesting," came a voice. I rolled over to see Jock crouching by my side, already dressed.

I looked around. Most of the men were still passed out.

"How?" I asked Jock.

"Air strikes."

"Not here," I said, sitting up and grabbing my boots and socks. "I don't hear anything. Incoming?"

"Nope, not here," Jock said. "They hit the capital."

"The imperials hit Corwistal?"

"No, the Corwies are hitting the Ulimba-Mor. Come on, try to keep up."

"Dude, I just woke up." I shook my head to get the cobwebs out. "Run that by me again."

"The King of Corwistal heard about his son getting whacked and hit back at the Ulimbese."

"Yeah, I don't blame him. I would be pissed too," I said. "Do the Corwies know it was us?"

"I dunno," Jock said. "Though if they find out, they're gonna be pissed at us too."

I shrugged. "What are they gonna do about it? Their army is just slightly more competent than a gang of kids with sticks."

"Hey, don't get too cocky," Jock frowned, shaking his head. "Even a kid with a stick can beat your head in."

A couple other guys were waking up now and listening in. Four-eyes had showed up behind me. "You know, Sarge," he said quietly, "the imperials may retaliate if they are mad enough at us."

"Like how?" said Jock. "Lodge a formal protest with the colonel? About what, killing too many of their enemies? Performing our contract too well?"

He shook his head. "I'm not sure you're thinking this through, Jock. We're sitting here without armor, artillery, or proper supplies in the middle of enemy territory, and our friends don't seem to like us all that much."

"Maybe," Jock said. "But without us, their offensive would have stalled out. They know we pulled their imperial chestnuts out of the fire."

Four-eyes nodded. "Sure, but we'd better have an alternative in mind. Just in case."

"Yeah," I said. "Seems reasonable to me."

Jock punched me in the arm. "All right, boys. But before we do that, we need to know what's going on, and we aren't going to do that by sitting around here. I'm going to liberate some coffee from command HQ and hang out over there to see what happens next."

"Want some company?" I said.

"Sure," said Jock. "Just keep your mouth shut. What about you, Four-eyes? Coming?"

He shook his head. "I'm going to hit up Andrews and see if I can jack into local radio chatter."

"Good idea," Jock said. "Let's go, Tommy."

The command tent was rather more decorative than any I'd seen before. Scratch that. It was downright gaudy. The colonel had gotten it from the Ulimbese, since our stuff was still lost in shipping limbo. The thing looked like it was requisitioned from a gaudy, low-end whorehouse. It had gold, green, and red stripes with an upside-down ice cream cone top. I admit, I laughed when I saw it. But I kept it in. Mostly.

Major Skelton was pacing outside the tent when we showed up. I'd served with him a few times, but he and Jock went way back.

"Major," Jock said, and Skelton nodded at him. "Good to see you, Sergeant. Looks like our friendlies might not be feeling so friendly."

"Yeah," said Jock, "so I've heard. Any idea where we can get some coffee around here, Major?"

Skelton raised an eyebrow. "If you're looking for a waitress, you've come to the wrong place. However, if corporal might be able to liberate some from back there," he jerked a finger towards a smaller tent. "Bring three cups. Major's orders."

I saluted, fetched the coffee, then returned as directed. It smelled better than anything I'd had in a while. Probably an officer's private stash.

"The airstrikes didn't take out the emperor, fortunately, but the Corwies were clearly NOT kidding around. Stratarches Tark is probably going to show up any second now and start screaming about it." Major Skelton was telling Jock. "I don't know how much they know about our real client."

"They know something," said Jock, sipping at his coffee. "Everyone knows we're not just here for an imperial real estate acquisition program."

As we spoke, Colonel Emerson himself stepped outside the tent, looking pained, followed by his aide, an Ulimbese liaison, and a captain from Echo Company. We saluted and he returned the salute, then signed off on something his aide was presenting to him.

"Major," he said. "I may need you for something in a few minutes." Then he noticed what we were drinking. "Is that my coffee?"

"Yes sir," the major replied calmly.

"Damn your eyes, then." He nodded to Jock in silent approval; clearly he wasn't about to say anything about the previous night's operation in front of the imperial officer.

"Sir!" a lieutenant called out.

"Yes?" said the colonel.

"Stratarches Tark will be here in a few minutes. SOG monitored his vehicle approaching the perimeter."

The colonel nodded and sighed. "Well, Major," he said. "Looks like we'll get to exercise our diplomacy this morning."

A few minutes later, Stratarches Tark marched in accompanied by a gaggle of highly-decorated, high-ranking imperial officers. His face was red and angry.

"Colonel Emerson," he barked without introduction. "As you know, I am a member of the Imperial Family of Ulimba-Mor, the very family that has been savagely attacked by the Corwistalian air forces thanks to your brash and foolish action!"

The colonel's face was a mask of polite indifference. "An action which you knew was forthcoming."

"That is beside the point," the man growled. "My uncle, the glorious Emperor of Ulimba-Mor, may he live forever, suffered his own imperial palace being struck by no less than four Corwistalian missiles. The damage is extensive—we were unprepared—you should have consulted with us about the timing of your action!"

"I offer my condolences for the losses you have sustained," the colonel responded calmly. "However, your inability to defend your capital city or the imperial palace against an enemy airstrike is not my problem, nor is it one of our contractual obligations."

"Yes it is," the Stratarches said. "It absolutely is now! The emperor is ordering you to strike back against these vile Corwistalians in reprisal." He nodded to one of his aides and the man handed him a data pad. "Here, this is the location of the airbase from which the assault was launched. We are within a day's march of it."

The colonel sighed and shook his head. "No, Stratarches, we are not going to strike back."

"Why?" the Stratarches spluttered. "This is your fault!"

The colonel said nothing.

"Does it look too hard for you!?" Stratarches Tark spat. "Can you not manage to call out your drones? Are your men too tired?"

"We're not going to strike back," the colonel repeated.

"I cannot believe what I'm hearing," Tark raged. "You have been supplied by us, you are in our employ, you are here to wage war on behalf of the Emperor, and yet, when he calls upon you, you dare to refuse him?"

"The Emperor is your commander, not ours," the colonel replied calmly. "And without the Wardogs, your armor would be scattered in pieces across the Apis valley and your base there would have fallen to the Corwistalians. I understand your desire to seek vengeance. But we simply cannot participate at this juncture."

"We will strike back against the king's forces, with or without you. And if you do not participate in this operation, you will not participate in anything else," the stratarches declared angrily. "I will see that you and your men leave this camp today, and take nothing of ours with you. You can find your own food and supplies. Perhaps the

Corwistalians will take pity on you. I'm not warning you, Colonel! I will do it!"

The stratarches spat on the ground in front of the colonel, spun on his heel and walked away, his followers with him.

"Excitable fellow," the colonel muttered, then turned back into the tent.

"Well," Jock mused out loud, "Tark was sure peeved. If we get cut off from local slop, I think I'm going to find myself a wing joint to loot."

"Ah," said Major Skelton, "speaking of looting, I guess you missed the good stuff going around last night."

"What?" said Jock. "Hey, did you guys get into the palace without me?"

The major shrugged. "Let's just say a few of the boys who were a little closer to our Ulimbese allies hit the royal cellar."

"Dammit," said Jock. "Did they drink it dry?"

"Pretty damn close," the major said. "If you're lucky someone might have saved a bottle of something."

"Come to think of it," I said, "everyone did seem to be sleeping in this morning."

"Great," said Jock. "I hope we get paid well for our field trip. I could use a stiff one. And a smoke. Do the Ulimbese smoke?"

The major shrugged. "Not that I've seen, but the royalty might have some tobacco on him."

"Ah well," said Jock. "Come on, Tommy. Let's get out of here before the colonel remembers his coffee."

That sounded like a good idea to me. The colonel was like the god of war. Angering gods was bad for mercenaries.

I looked around our new digs. The girl in the fountain was still spitting water, though now she had a hovertank parked next to her. Our new base was sprawled across the lawn of the palace. The Ulimbese had taken the royal building for themselves, but we had our own tent city going across the lawn and some of the outbuildings. Our new "barracks," where I'd slept the night before, were a large barn. We didn't all fit and the overflow was scattered around containers and other outbuildings. The base was obviously still in progress.

My biggest concern was finding the mess tent at this point.

"A drink and a smoke," Jock said, "then some target practice."

"I don't get you," I said, "you eat like a girl but you've got no problem drinking and smoking."

Jock looked at me with a frown. "You stupid, Tommy? Don't you understand balance?"

"Balance?" I said.

"Yeah. You eat well, then you can smoke and drink. You eat crap and smoke and drink, you die. You eat healthy, then you can smoke and drink all you want. It all balances out."

"I don't think it works that way," I said.

"Yeah, well you don't understand how the body works. You're just lucky that someone will shoot you in the head long before your arteries are clogged."

We found the mess tent and a couple of older local women heaped portions on our plates. It was some sort of roots in a gravy. Not my first choice for breakfast, but I was famished. I topped off my coffee cup from a big metal carafe and found the brew to be better than expected. The Ulimbese or Corwistalians or someone must grow the stuff.

Park joined Jock and me a couple minutes after we sat down. He had a sly grin on his face but wouldn't say why. I figured he'd gotten some of the local brandy and didn't want to share. Bastard.

"Yo," came a voice. It was Ace. "Long time no see," he said, sitting down with his plate. On top of his roots he had some shredded cheese.

"Cheese?" Park said. "Where did you get that?"

Ace shrugged and tucked in.

And then we heard the sound of that Ulimbese tube drum howling and battering away.

"What the hell?" someone muttered.

Jock nodded his head. "They're gonna hit back."

"Yep," I said.

"Hit where?" Ace asked.

"Corwistalian base."

Then Four-eyes joined us and Jock turned to him. "Isn't that right, Four-eyes?"

"Yes," he said. "The base is about 30 kilometers from here. My bet is they'll send in some troops and mortar it. Corwistalians have little in the way of armor and not enough guys holding the base."

"It would be fun to drone it," Park said around a mouthful of potatoes.

"Yeah," I said, "but the major said no. Not our objective. We're just hanging around for now. Hurry up and wait."

"So," Jock said to Four-eyes, "when are the Ulimbese mounting their assault?"

"Not sure," said Four-eyes. "Right now they're just on alert and readying equipment. Nothing else on the chatter."

I finished my roots and decided to go back for more, then found a confrontation at the head of the line.

"Hey," a private was telling one of the local serving women, "come on, I'm starving here."

"Nothing else," she said. "We're done!"

"Done?" I said, "what do you mean you're done?"

"They told us to stop, then took the food," she said. "Sorry. We're just cleaning up now."

"Who? What?" I said, then looked back. "Hey Jock—the Ulimbese just took the rest of the food."

"St. Possenti kick their puckered asses," Jock swore. "What is this crap?"

"Stratarches Tark being pissy," I said.

Just then Ward and Leighton walked in, still bleary eyed. "I could kill for some scrambled eggs," Leighton said.

"You'll have to," Jock said. "The diner is now closed."

"Closed?" said Ward. "You kidding us?"

"I wish," I said. "I was really hoping for a second plate of delicious boiled roots."

And then, in walked Major Skelton. The few dozen men stood and saluted and he saluted back briskly.

"Listen, men—we have an issue. Colonel wants everyone. Command tent. Now."

We filed out after him. The beating of the Ulimbese instruments had stopped. I glanced across the gardens as we headed towards the colonel. The Ulimbese were in formation near the castle, and more men were on top of a balcony. Looked like an address was taking place but I couldn't hear anything from here.

We reached the tent and I saw a lot of guys squinting and holding their heads. They had definitely drunk all the good stuff, the greedy pigs.

We gathered together as best as we could in the parking lot containing the command tent. I caught quite a few questioning eyes and shrugs.

About five minutes later, the colonel walked out of the tent, flanked by Lt. Colonel Adams.

"Good morning, men," he said, looking us over. "We've hit a potential snag and we're going to un-snag it before it turns into a tear."

He stopped and looked towards the palace grimly, then continued. "As most of you probably know by now, there was a Corwistalian airstrike at 0600 this morning. A wing of fighters came in low and sent missiles directly into the Imperial palace. These fighters originated from an airbase located some thirty kilometers from here. After the raid, I was approached by Stratarches Tark about launching a strike on the base. This, however, does not fit with our primary objective and we have refused his request. Now, unfortunately, our erstwhile allies have decided to play politics with our logistical support, threatening to cut us off completely. As HQ is still unable to get us proper supplies, this is endangering not only our mission, but our men. If we are not supplied and the Corwistalians attack, we're at a disadvantage. Granted, it's not a disadvantage you men could not overcome, but I still believe we should have every advantage. For now, cause the Ulimbese no reason for dislike and perform your duties for the day as normal. If food is lacking, stick to our supply of MREs and don't cause trouble. I've already been apprised of the mess hall situation. Just be ready for action—we're working out a plan and hope to restore logistical support by tomorrow at the latest. Dismissed."

"MREs, great," Ward said.

I laughed. "Actually, Private, they're slightly better than the boiled roots."

"Yeah, maybe," he said, "but I would have liked a chance to compare the two."

I went back to barracks, borrowed a reader and kicked my feet up with a book for all of ten minutes before deciding I couldn't live with myself anymore unless I got a shower. I asked around and found that some of the guys had run some hoses from concealed spigots in the garden and threw up some plastic tarps over trellises to make an outdoor shower. No one seemed to have any soap but it was better than nothing. The cold water was bracing.

I made my way back to barracks after dressing in my filthy clothes again, then kicked back with the book. The day crawled along into the evening. I can't remember what I did the rest of that day but it sure as heck seemed like it took up a week. A week of waiting. I was itching to see what might be planned for the evening. Scuttlebutt had revealed nothing of restoration of logistical support by the Ulimbese or of any clever plans by the colonel.

And then, around 10PM, just as I was thinking of hitting the sack, Jock showed up.

"We're moving, Corporal Falkland."

"Moving?" I said.

"Operation Five-Finger is underway and you've been tapped."

"Awesome," I said, grabbing my gear. "Who needs sleep?"

A few minutes later my squad was gathered around the nude fountain girl. I was kind of getting fond of her at this point. Ward, Leighton, me, Park, Four-eyes, Jock and Ace were there.

"Listen, men," Jock said. "Colonel is done with this Ulimbese passive-aggressive crap. We're taking matters into our own hands. As of 0930, Stratarches Tark ordered about ¾ of the Ulimbese off to go shell the airbase. He's up in the palace with his boys and we've got them outnumbered. So we're taking what we need for now, damn the consequences, then moving camp to separate from the Ulimbese force."

"Sir," said Four-eyes.

"Yes?"

"The Ulimbese have both armor and multiple gunships. We may have more men and experience, but we're heavily out-gunned if they decide to—"

Jock waved his hand. "Do you think the colonel is an idiot, Raymond?"

"No sir," said Four-eyes. "I just—"

"Shut your mouth, genius," Jock said. "We're the ones in charge of taking down the enemy gunships."

"Explosives," Park said, his eyes lighting up.

"No explosives," said Jock firmly. "We're not going to blow them up. We just need to keep them out of the air long enough to keep the Ulimbese from chasing us."

"Cross the cables," said Ace.

"Say what?" said Jock.

"I've flown these things," Ace said. "Get inside the casing, under the second rotor, switch a few cables around, they'll short the hell out when they ramp up for takeoff."

"Great," said Jock, "you're hired. I thought we'd just hacksaw through various bits and hope for the best, but I think I like your plan better."

Ace grinned. "No problem."

"Leighton, Park, Ward, you guys are in charge of taking out the sentries and the lights," Jock said. "I don't want you killing anyone if you don't have to. This is a non-lethal operation. You do understand what that means, right?"

"Kill them nicely?" Park asked, with an innocent expression.

"Just don't kill anyone," Jock said. "Unless you really have to. The Ulimbese are already upset with us, we don't want them out for blood."

"Copy that, sir," I said. And the lieutenant was right. We had enough trouble on our hands already, we didn't need to go looking for more.

"Treadwell, you are our saboteur. Falkland and I will be your cover. Four-eyes, you are to stay concealed along the path and watch for incoming reinforcements.

The hike to the field where the gunship squadron sat took about twenty minutes. We acted casual, as if out for a stroll. That is, until we heard the far-off sound of breaking glass and sirens behind us and figured the cat was out of the bag. Some of our boys were wreaking havoc back at the palace. I hoped they liberated some more brandy.

We ducked low and kept our eyes open for Ulimbese. A few passed us but they were running back towards the palace and paid us no mind. The moon was not working to our advantage. It hung big and blue in the sky, flickering through the branches of the orchard through which we walked quietly along the edge of a path. Four-eyes stopped and melted into the night. I saw a yellow glow ahead. The lights of the landing area. We continued until we reached the edge of the orchard. I looked across the close-cropped grass to a small airfield, likely intended for private aircraft and visitors to the royal family. There were scattered clouds above, but nothing we could count on. I saw a few light craft and private jets, then further out I made out a dozen gunships hulking on the pavement, casting black shadows beneath the buzzing lights on poles. I had a crazy memory of cow-tipping and almost laughed. The more things changed....

Jock nodded at Park and he left around the edge of the airfield with Leighton and Ward. From where we were I spotted one sentry, sitting in the back of a hoverjeep near a transformer. Around the sulphur-yellow lights insects swirled as he looked down at a pad. Probably playing a game of solitaire. Or texting some girl.

Park walked up briskly behind the man, just like he owned the place. The soldier turned and jumped to get out but Park caught him with a blow to the chin with the heel of his hand, knocking the man out, then folded him down into the back of the vehicle. Then Leighton and Ward set a charge at the base of the transformer, then the three of them walked casually away. About 100 meters to our left was a hangar with a few men hanging around. They looked like techs, not soldiers. Maybe even civilian. They didn't seem to notice anything.

A moment later, there was an explosion and a burst of sparks. The main lights went out and the only remaining illumination was the emergency lights coming on inside the hangar, along with the solar-charged lights on the runway. Our team was on.

We raced towards the first of the gunships and gave Ace a boost onto the wing where he worked on ratcheting open an access panel. About three minutes later, I heard the panel open, then the sound of heavy wire snips clipping cables. Another two minutes and I heard the panel close, then he jumped down.

"11 more to go," he said, and we moved to the next aircraft. Up to the wing, pop the panel, fiddle in the guts, then down again. This time he did it in about four minutes.

And then we went to the third aircraft. We boosted Ace up onto the wing and he went to work. Then, a moment later, the cabin door swung open and a man shouted at us. The pilot!

"Shut up!" I shouted, pointing my rifle at him. He threw his hands up just as a scream echoed from inside the gunship. I swore. It was a girl. She stuck her head out from behind the pilot and he snapped at her, then looked at us. "What the devil do you think you're doing?"

"Routine inspection," Jock said from behind me, his rifle now aimed as well.

The pilot narrowed his eyes at us. "You're not inspectors. You're offworlders!"

"Yeah, well, you'd be advised to play along anyhow, flyboy," Jock said. "How about you and your lady friend step on down nice and slow."

The pilot grimaced, then started to climb down. In a moment, he was standing beside us. Then it was the girl's turn.

"Come on down, sweetheart," Jock said. "Nice and slow."

She did, shaking and sniffling. Nice legs, though.

"Now," Jock said to me, "zip 'em up."

I grabbed a few zip ties from my pack and moved towards the ill-fated lovers. The woman was dressed in a short white skirt and a tight top that showed her nice flat belly. I could smell her perfume as I reached for her wrist.

Then the pilot made a stupid grab for my rifle. Jock shot him in the arm, spinning him around and knocking him to the pavement. Jock put the barrel of his gun to the man's head and the guy went stock-still, gasping in pain. Then the girl screamed, which startled me, so I punched her in the face. She went down like a sack of flour.

"Dude," said Ace from the wing. "You're not supposed to hit girls."

I shrugged, then zip-tied the two of them to one of the landing struts. "You...bastards..." gasped the pilot.

"Tell her I didn't mean it when she wakes up," I said, by way of apology. "We're just a little bit jumpy."

Then I heard further noises from the cabin of the gunship. It sounded like people talking. Jock cocked his head as well. A conversation. And then the tinny sound of gunfire. I laughed and climbed the ladder, retrieving a tablet, still playing a movie, and held it up to show Ace and Jock. Inside the cabin was a half-empty bottle of wine and a bag of some kind of orange corn puffs. I rolled the top down and stuffed it in my pack. You never know when you might need some corn puffs.

"Seems we interrupted date night," I said to Jock as Ace jumped down off the wing.

"Yeah," he said. "Looks like it." He looked down at the bleeding man. "We should probably kill him. Hell, the Ulimbese will probably shoot him anyway when they see him here with the girl, assuming he was on guard duty."

"You know," I said, "I kind of feel bad for the idiot. This is a backwater, not a lot of entertainment here."

"True," said Ace, looking down at the girl. "And as one player to another, this guy has decent taste in woman."

"Listen," said the pilot through gritted teeth. "If you leave her here...leave us here...they'll execute me. And who knows what they'll do to her..."

"Tell you what," Jock said. "We'll hide the evidence by taking the rest of your booze, then leave the girl someplace safe."

"You won't rape her?" said the pilot.

"Don't insult us," said Ace. "We're professionals. Gentleman mercenaries, you might say."

The pilot nodded towards the girl. "Is she okay?" he said.

I checked her pulse. Steady, though she'd be feeling that hit for days. "She'll live."

Jock pulled out a strip of bandage and wrapped it around the pilot's arm. "No hard feelings," he said, before he cracked the guy in the back of the head with the butt of his rifle.

I grabbed the wine bottle and Jock threw the girl over his shoulder. A moment later we were joined by our second team. Leighton and Park took the girl over to the jeep with the unconscious sentry and dumped her in the back next to him.

"This is taking too long," Jock said. "Park, watch Ace on the fourth gunship, then do whatever he's doing."

"Short on tools," Ace said.

I jogged over to the jeep, found a toolbox and brought it back to the team. Ace rooted through it and pulled out a screwdriver and a wrench. "Close enough," he said. "This will do. You can use your combat knife to cut the wires, Park. Come on."

We followed them, leaving Leighton behind to watch the girl and the felled security guy.

The rest of the sabotage went off without a hitch. As we got to the last one, I looked in an almost empty hanger and spotted an unattended hoverjeep on my thermals.

"Hey boss," I said to Jock, "can you spare me for a minute?"

He nodded and I jogged over to the hangar. It was pitch black and I could see the engine of the jeep was still warm from having been run within the last few hours. Good, it was working then. To my great delight, the keys were in the ignition.

This was really turning out to be easier than it should have been, but that was all the fault of the Ulimbese. Their perimeter was about a kilometer out. Last thing they figured was that someone inside that guarded line was going to be fiddling with their stuff. I cranked the engine and the skirting of the jeep rose from the floor. It was almost like antigrav or like taking a flat-bottom boat out on a lake. You just glide over everything. As a bonus, the jeep had a mounted gun and some ammo in it. Life was good. I cruised up to the last gunship as the men jumped down from the wing.

Jock looked at me and the jeep and grinned. "Nice," he said. "Shotgun!"

I laughed and the guys jumped in, then we headed back to join Leighton and our accidental prisoners. When I got there, a couple of the guys jumped out and joined Leighton. And then we saw someone walking rapidly across the tarmac in the near darkness towards us. "Evening," he said. "Did you happen to–" then he stopped, realizing we weren't Ulimbese—and that we had our rifles out. Another pilot.

He stood there dumbly staring at us. Jock sighed. "Alright, flyboy," he said, "obviously you've stumbled on something that shouldn't be happening. Thing is, if you yell, we'll kill you. And we're not here to kill anyone, you understand?"

The man had now seen the two people in the back of the jeep. "But—"

"They are not dead," Jock assured him. "And you won't be either if you do what I say."

The man nodded.

"Great," Jock said, indicating Ward. "This nice man here is going to walk you over to that storage bay, then you are going to get inside and get down on the ground and stay there until you count to five thousand. If you make any noise or try to open the door too soon, I swear to Possenti we will blow your idiot brains out. Got it?"

The pilot nodded again and Ward led him to the bay, put him inside, then pulled down the slotted metal door and tied a piece of cordage through the lock hole.

Then he jogged back to us and we crammed ourselves into the jeep. We drove back up the path, pausing to pick up Four-eyes. He jumped on the back bumper and tossed a Ulimbese cap into the front seat.

"Where's the rest of the guy?" I said.

He shrugged. "Probably still running."

Then, up ahead, I saw multiple sets of headlights. "Off the road!" Jock said, and I took the hoverjeep right into the woods as Park did the same with his jeep. Surprisingly, the weird vehicle handled the rough transition perfectly. I could get used to this thing.

Then there was a moan from behind me. It was the sentry. Jock pushed his gun barrel into the man's chest and made a shushing sound. The guy looked confused as he realized there was also an unconscious girl sprawled across him.

Then the vehicles passed us—a few trucks heading to the airfield. They didn't spot us but we stayed put as we heard more movement along the dark path. A handful of Ulimbese, jogging through the darkness towards the airfield, among them multiple pilots. Then another truck.

At that point, the lights went on at the airfield. Must have sprung the backup breaker.

We watched the road for a couple of minutes and saw nothing more, so we jumped back on and headed to base.

There we found an absolute mess. Colonel Emerson had established a perimeter around the barracks, the mess hall and the command tent. Meanwhile, troops were unloading bags of roots and grains, ammo and various goods from a truck with inexplicably flat tires, while others faced a disorganized mob of Ulimbese, while a sergeant with a bullhorn yelled that the goods were being requisitioned in the name of the Emperor and the imperial war effort.

We explained the unexpected prisoner situation to Captain Marks and he handed them over to a couple of privates for safe keeping. They grinned at the girl, who was now conscious and cursing everyone in sight, only taking breaks every now and then to plead for permission to talk to her father. I'm didn't see what good her father was going to do in the face of an entire mercenary company, even one as lightly armed as we were, but she was cute and we enjoyed her harmless ranting.

Before long, we were ordered to move out and occupy a sprawling neighborhood and sports field a little ways outside the palace grounds, nearer to the airfield where we'd just been.

We moved out, taking our ill-gotten loot with us. A posh hotel was commandeered for a barracks and a couple of nearby buildings were set up as command posts. We had a solid perimeter set up within half an hour, though clearing the few civilians in the area out took some time and apologies. We were very nice, I'd say. I don't think we even had to break any arms or jaws.

I didn't have to deal with weeping hotel denizens, however. The Sergeant on Guard sent our squad up on a roof with a radio to watch the road back to the palace. I parked my jeep in the hotel parking lot and took the keys with me. No sense in letting some other soldier take my sweet ride. We parked the other jeep next to it. Now we had a grand total of two vehicles, unless the colonel had managed to free any others from the Ulimbese.

"The Stratarches must be pissed," Park said to me from his perch behind a big industrial AC unit, "over under on how long it takes to call in a strike on us?"

"I dunno," I said. "I doubt he'd try it."

"Crow One, this is Kilo One," came Captain Marks's voice over the radio. Jock picked up. "Crow One, I read you Kilo One."

"Hope you achieved strategic objective, Crow One. We've got activity at the airfield."

"Roger that."

We looked down towards the light of the airfield and saw the rotors start to spin with our hearts in our mouths. Faster, and faster, then—POP! We saw the light of a small explosion on the side of one craft—then another—then a string of 'em, followed by the pop of small explosions. Ace grinned ear to ear.

Yeah, gotta love success. I pulled out the corn puffs and passed them around along with the half-bottle of wine. As the pink fingers of dawn stretched across the sky, we munched contemplatively and took swigs while we waited to see if the Ulimbese would try a ground strike.

Nope, not that dumb. All in all, it was a great night. And tomorrow, we should have some breakfast. Emerson was a cold-blooded bastard but he loved his men. Tark had no idea who he was pushing.

Chapter 8

In Too Deep

You know, you don't really think laundry is a big deal until you spend a few days sweating through a uniform you can't change without going naked.

The hotel had a great laundry facility, though, and I was pleased as punch to send my one-and-only uniform through while I took a shower, then lounged around in a towel with my borrowed e-reader.

Park and Ace had set up a game system in the pair of rooms we were splitting and were noisily machine-gunning guys. You laugh, but I'll tell you what: the best way to unwind from shooting lots of people in real life is to shoot them on the screen.

Getting set up in a decent location with some secure supplies made me feel better about this mission. I still wasn't sure exactly what our final objective was, but I was pretty sure it had something to do with that cargo freighter we nabbed, not this petty war between two backward nation-states.

Jock wandered into the room hauling two 20 kilo dumbbells. "Lookee I found," he announced, curling one of them.

"Where'd you find those?" Four-eyes said, looking over from the desk where he was perusing local news on his tablet.

"Gym downstairs," Jock said, putting the weights by the bed.

"Ah," said Four-eyes, going back to his reading.

"Well, Tommy," Jock said, punching me in the arm. "You feel like taking a ride in your hoverjeep and hunting down a liquor store?"

I shook my head. "I don't think I'd like to wander around town all that much. Better to stay on base. Ulimbese aren't happy with us and I'm sure the Corwistalians aren't either."

"Aw, they'll forget soon enough," Jock said. "Especially with us being so handsome." He paused and looked thoughtful. "Come to think of it, though—we may have to go foraging sooner rather than later. And not just for liquor."

"Yeah?" I said. "I thought we got a huge load of stuff from the Ulimbese."

"We did, but not as much as you might think when you divide it across a battalion of guys. Scuttlebutt is we're going to run out in a few days."

"Great," I said. "And no word on our own supply line?"

"No," Four-eyes chimed in. "Litigation is in progress, or some such nonsense. Our stock price has gone down eight percent over the last week. Someone leaked to investors."

"If we go below 200-day moving average I'm selling," Park said.

"There goes my cushy retirement," Ace said, jabbing buttons down as he machine-gunned a squad of laser-spraying xenos inside a dark warehouse.

"So what's going to happen?" I asked Jock. "Are we gonna get help from the Ulimbese again."

"Probably," he said. "They're talking. General Stratarchy or whatever his name is overreached a bit. Apparently the Empire isn't happy with us but they never authorized cutting us off."

"Yeah," said Park. "We should kick everyone's ass on this whole planet."

"Not without supplies," Four-eyes said. "Or higher tech."

"You're no fun," Park said, then killed another half-dozen people with a flamethrower.

Jock's intuition on the Ulimbese was right, though. They did decide to back us up again. And of course, it didn't work nicely. Instead, it was a total clusterfrag.

I mean, it started normally enough. "We're gonna have a drop come in, countryside where we don't risk any hand-held surface to air," they told us. Then they said, "We'll send a squad to retrieve it, real quiet like." Then it was "And that's you."

And "Since you found a couple of hoverjeeps, you see our reasoning."

And now I was driving through the countryside with nine other Wardogs.

The drop was tagged with an encoded beacon we could track. The hoverjeeps let us roll over land and water, though they were sketchy when you got into brush or really rocky areas.

The weather was idyllic as we cruised along on a sunny morning. Four-eyes was watching his tablet and giving me directions. Behind me was the second jeep. Other than Four-eyes, I had Leighton, Jones and Park. Jones had recovered from his concussion nicely and insisted no one was going to cut him out of his share of the action.

"We're getting close, Falkland," Four-eyes reported, pointing towards the gently rolling peak of a nearby hill. "Should be just on the other side there."

I followed his finger and readjusted. Floating over the grass was novel. We went up and over the hill, then down again. Behind me, the second jeep followed, a good 50 meters back.

"Where is that thing?" I asked, looking down at the sloping grassland below but not seeing the cargo.

"Should be more than one thing," Four-eyes said. "A collection of things."

Then I saw them. A string of lumps sticking out on the next hillside. The parachutes were pale green, as were the packages. They were big, too. The size of small shipping containers, with bolts of fabrics draped around them.

It made sense to pick this area. It was some sort of national park with no local population, except for campers and hikers. Of those, we'd seen no sign. Camping probably lost its appeal when your nation was invaded.

I pulled up and parked, then the second hoverjeep did the same. Out stepped Jock, Ace, Ward, Leighton and Corporal Howland. I missed Rocky, dammit.

I watched as Four-eyes scanned and inventoried the cargo. Ace, Leighton, Ward and Park set up a perimeter at four corners. We'd switch later, but for the next six hours I had nothing to do. I still remember the sound of the birds, the warm breeze, the fluffy clouds overhead.

And then Jock's radio burst to life, along with the chatter of gunfire somewhere just out of sight.

"Incoming," yelled Ace. "From the East. I'm under fire—I'm–"

Then the radio went dead. I was on my feet as soon as I heard the gunfire. My first thought was to go get Ace—and Jock had the same idea.

"Four-eyes," he said, "keep working. Jones, keep him covered. Howland, get in–" he pointed to the hoverjeep. I didn't need telling. I was already in the driver's seat and firing up the blowers.

There was very little cover so I simply headed east with little thought of tactical advantage. As we got up the side of the hill I heard gunfire being exchanged. "Hold on, Ace," I said. "We're coming."

We hit the top of the hill. *POW!* A round slammed into the door beside me and I just about flipped the damn jeep jerking the wheel back. Jock opened up with an explosion of automatic fire, aiming down the hillside. "I spot three," he yelled, then sent another burst of fire. I saw them too. Corwistalian regulars. They'd hit the ground already and were sending rounds past us. I slammed the jeep into reverse so we were just behind the ridge of the hill.

"We gotta crawl over," I announced, shutting off the engine. Jock nodded. Jones and Howland jumped out of the back and we went on our bellies to the edge of the hill. The slow curve wasn't great for cover. "We also gotta spread out," Howland said, chewing a toothpick. "Agreed," Jock said. "Falkland and I go over here, 5 meters apart. You go left, Jones go right."

I heard the chatter of more gunfire. "Where the devil is Ace?" I shouted to Jock as we crept forward.

"Holed up behind a boulder," Jock said. "Let's nail the bastards."

We crested the hill and opened up. The men shot towards us but were retreating. It was long range. Probably 400 meters. I switched off automatic and sighted in. *CRACK*—I sent a round, and a miss. Then another. I heard shots from either side of me. Jones and Howland. Then the chatter of full auto fire again sent my eyes down. Ace was behind a small boulder about 50 meters down the hill. He was bleeding—I could see it from here.

I sighted in again—and the men were running now, looking for cover. I fired and one went down—but I heard Jones shoot at the same time, so I wasn't sure who got the kill.

Suddenly, there was a huge *THUMP* and a big chunk of ground shot dirt all over Jock and I as something slammed into the hillside below us.

"Artillery!" Jones yelled, pointing towards a patch of woods. There, just emerging—a hovertank. Great.

"We gotta get Ace," I said, not waiting for a reply. "Cover me!"

I ran down to where Ace was now trying to stand. Our original assailants were out of sight now.

"Ace!" I said. "Come on up—I got the jeep."

He shook his head. "Can't stand. Hit."

I reached him and helped him up. He had a nasty hit to the thigh.

"Radio box smashed," he said, pointing to its remains. "Through radio, into leg," he said through gritted teeth.

Jock was there now, taking Ace's other arm.

THUMP—CRACK!

Another tank round impacted near us, throwing dirt in a huge spray. Time to MOVE!

"Blue one, this is Yellowstone," Jock's radio crackled with Park's voice, "Enemy spotted, 1000 meters. From the South. At least a company."

"Roger that, Yellowstone. All men, return," Jock said as we moved. "We're bringing in Ace now. He's wounded. Over." He switched channels. Crow One to Kilo One, we're under attack here. We have at least one advancing tank. We have been compromised. Need medical, one wounded."

"We hear you Crow One," came a calm voice. "Hold out for reinforcements. Over."

And then another shell hit, throwing us to the ground in a hail of dirt. Ace yelled in pain as he fell on his wounded leg. Jock and I were back up quickly and we hauled him over the hill and into the jeep. "We need those reinforcements sooner not later, Kilo One. Over."

"Roger that," came the voice. "Will give you an ETA when available, over."

Jones and Howland pulled back and joined us, then I gunned it back to the cargo drop site.

Four-eyes was looking at his tablet in frustration.

"We're missing a couple," he said as Jock jumped out of the jeep. "My guess is back in the woods somewhere."

"What do you have so far?" Jock said. "Anything we can use against a tank?"

"A tank?" Four-eyes said, looking up in dismay. "You can't be serious."

Jock nodded.

"Geez," Four-eyes said, looking down his list as he stood between two containers on a pile of fabric. "I'd like to tell you we've got a cruise missile in here, but I'm having some issues reading the Ulimbese coding system properly. I think these are food," he pointed at a few entries on the screen as Jock peered at the unfamiliar script, "and this is probably ammo, judging by the numbers. Weight numbers are galactic standard, but this scribbly crap the locals call writing isn't helpful. My AI would have translated already, but..."

"Tech 10, I know," Jock said impatiently. "Listen, there's a tank coming over the hill in a few minutes. Maybe more than one. Leighton, you're scout—radio in when they get close. Everyone else, stick here. Raymond, do all the containers have beacons?"

"No," said Four-eyes. "There's the central one—that's got the beacon—then there was a web of filament that was supposed to keep the falling containers together. Obviously, some of them broke away."

"We're supposed to have more RPGs, aren't we? In one of these?"

"Yeah," Four-eyes said. "But there are twelve containers here. And six more scattered who knows where."

"Tommy," Howland said, "help me out here." He was cutting off the leg of Ace's pants beside one of the cargo containers.

"You just want to see my thigh," Ace hissed, trying to joke through the pain.

"I want to see you live. Get pressure on this wound," Howland said, handing me a wad of gauze.

The wound was ugly. A large chunk was taken out of the top of his left thigh. A piece of radio casing was embedded a little lower. Blood leaked from the gash in small pulses with the rhythm of his heart.

"Femoral?" Ace said.

Howland shook his head. "Looks like a miss."

"Lucky," Ace said.

I pressed the gauze in and held it fast. Ace took a hissing intake of breath but said nothing. Howland quickly wrapped a tourniquet above the wound.

"Take out the plastic piece," Ace said, handing him his multitool.

"No can do," Howland said. "That might be keeping you from bleeding out. It'll have to wait." Howland poured in disinfectant, packed in more gauze, then taped up the wounds. "That's it for now," he said, putting his hand on Ace's shoulder. "I think you'll live."

"I'd better," Ace said, "or a lot of ladies are gonna came looking to take revenge on you, doc."

Our other patrols were back and casualty-free. Jock gathered us quickly. "They tracked the drop, boys. They know we're here, they know we need this. And they have at least one tank. Open these containers as fast as you can and search for anything we can use to blow it to hell."

"We're going to need a crowbar," Four-eyes said, using the word as if he'd always known it. I was already rifling through the toolbox in my jeep. I came out with a long screwdriver and a hammer. Jock grabbed the same and we raced to the first container and I started working at the thing. It had a lock of some sort that was supposed to be opened by some special tool. After a minute, I realized the hammer/screwdriver combo wasn't going to cut it.

"Clear out," I yelled, then fired a round into the lock. Still stuck. Then again. I hated doing that crap because of ricochets. The third round cracked the lock and I pried with the screwdriver as Ward and Jones pulled at the door. It let go, almost throwing us on the ground, and we were greeted with a flood of packing peanuts. Brushing them away I got to the cardboard and shrink-wrap covered boxes inside, then cut into the first one with my bayonet. A spurt of red startled me until I smelled tomato. Great. More lasagna.

"Next!" I yelled, and we started on the next container. *POW POW*—two shots this time, then prying it open, then another flood of packing peanuts. "Come on, Four-eyes," I said, throwing them away in fistfuls, "you really sure you don't know what's in these?"

"No," he said. "I got weights but not contents. That last one could have been one long gun or ten thousand blankets."

"Or a restaurant shipment," I said, as I cut into the first box I could reach. This one opened without damage and I hit something metal, and cut around it and got my hand into the dark box and around a cylinder. I pulled it out. It had a picture on the side. Loquats in syrup.

I threw it down and went to the next container, which was already being opened by Jones and Ward.

"Hey!" yelled Jock. "We got some ammo over here!"

"Great," I yelled back. "RPGs?"

"Negative," he said, "small arms."

"Then we have to keep–" Four-eyes said, then suddenly fell to the ground as I simultaneously heard the crack of a rifle. I hit the ground hard and heard the rattle of answering fire from behind another container. I didn't see the sniper—but I saw the pool of blood under Four-eyes and swore—he was dead. Right in the neck. GODDAM IT!

Ping-CRACK! I heard another bullet hit the container before the crack of the report. I sent a burst of fire up the field but still saw no-one. More answering fire rattled in my ears. Blood was rushing to my head as I went into the red zone—that madness you get under fire. Things slowed down as I spotted Ace behind the next container, rifle pointed over my head. He waved me in, and I ran in a crouch and hunkered down beside him.

"Ace," I said, "you good?"

"Yeah," he said, looking through his sight, rifle propped on his good knee. "I ain't moving, so they'd better get in sight. Yes…okay…there you go…right–" *CRACK!* He sent a round and I saw a man jump up in the grass, then fall again.

"That might be it," he said. "For the moment."

"Stay here and snipe," I said. All I could think about was hitting back. "I'm cracking cargo. Where the fuck did Leighton go?"

"TOMMY!" yelled Jock, "Over here!"

I ran three containers over to where he was pulling out a large wooden crate with Park's help. A bullet whizzed overhead. Park sent a burst of fire back as Jock and I ripped off the lid.

"Whoa," I said, realizing the interior of the box had multiple smaller boxes inside carefully nested in foam. I picked one up—it was really heavy. "What the devil are these?"

"Oh shit," said Jock. "There are nuke shells. Lead lined cases—made for a gun."

"What the hell–" I said, then two more bullets hit the ground in front of me.

"Next container," Jock yelled as we hit the ground and started crawling. "We can't launch those things anyhow."

Just as we got to the next container, there was a massive *THUMP!* and a crackling explosion of breaking glass and metal. I looked back—NO! MY JEEP!

A tank had crested the hill and blown up my goddamn jeep! Now I was pissed. I opened up with my rifle at the tank.

"Save your damn ammo!" Jock yelled at me.

"My JEEP!" I yelled back. "He blew up my goddam jeep!"

"Shut the hell up," Jock said, then yelled to the rest of the guys. "Back—get back! Tank incoming!"

THUMP-CRACK! A shell hit one of the containers near me, sending a massive splash of liquid up into the air. I suddenly smelled apples. Apple juice. Great.

"Get to the woods!" Jock yelled. Howland was hauling Ace by one arm. I grabbed the other and we hauled it towards the woods, half carrying our pilot.

The other guys were winging rounds back but I was too encumbered to use my rifle. 50 meters…40…meters…*THUMP!* A shell hit near us and threw us on the ground. Ace yelled in pain and I felt the sting of hot metal go into my right arm and neck. My ears were ringing. 35 meters to the woods. I pulled Ace up and Howland started to rise, then fell back to the ground and looked at me with a surprised expression as foam and blood poured from his mouth. "Howland!" I yelled, letting go of Ace and putting my hand on him. He looked up at me and said something that came out as a bubbling hiss, then his eyes went blank and a final breath rattled from his throat. He was gone—and I saw why, his jacket was soaked with blood. Chest hit.

"Dammit!" Ace yelled. "We gotta move!" I grabbed his arm but as we got up, *THUMP!* Another shell hit, knocking me on my ass. I looked back. Two tanks closing in, and at least a squad of guys coming over the top behind them. They'd spotted us and were closing in. "Come on!" I yelled, grabbing Ace and speeding him towards the woods. 20 meters, 10 meters—*THUMP—CRACK!* A tree in front of us blew into toothpicks, showering us with chips of wood as we closed in—and then were were in the woods. Ward grabbed Ace's other arm as we went further in. The woods were way too thin for my liking. Mostly regrowth with lots of space in between cover.

"Over here!" Jock yelled. "Another container!"

There, half hung up in a tree was another container. Jock blew the lock off and we started yanking out packaging. Medical supplies and linens. DAMMIT!

Bullets zipped over us and leaves fell from the trees. The tanks had stopped for the moment, but I knew we were going to be joined by Corwistalians in a moment.

Jock nodded at Park and he went up a tree to watch the mottled light at the entrance to the woods. I didn't see Jones anywhere.

I heard more gunfire behind us and whipped around. I couldn't see anything, but Jock tagged my arm and I went back to look.

As I tip-toed, I heard a grunt from a little ways ahead, then a "Eureka!"

"Jones!" I yelled.

"Falkland—get over here!"

He'd found another container and busted it open. "Here's the ticket!" he said, thumping the side of a long case. "120mm Mortar!"

"Run," I said to Jones. "Get the rest of the guys."

He ran back. I heard the rattling of guns off in the distance as I dug around for a crate of rounds.

A moment later, Jones was back, along with Jock. "Park and Ace are coming," Jock said, grabbing one end of a crate and throwing it out of the way. A bullet whizzed past us but we didn't dare shoot back, knowing our guys were still coming. I found a box of rounds and thanked Ares for his provision.

Park and Ace came up and Park dropped Ace next to a tree and lent his shoulder to the effort. As I pushed, I saw blood on the sleeve of my jacket. Shrapnel. Don't bleed to death now, I told myself as I pulled out rounds. I could hear the tank engines now. Way too close! "How the hell are we supposed to hit guys this close with a mortar?"

"Horizontal fire," Ace yelled, pain on his face. "Jam the baseplate against a tree or something, then throw the shell down the tube."

"I swear, if the bad guys don't kill us you guys will," Jock said.

"I'll load," Park said as we braced the mortar.

"Listen," Ace said, "you throw that round too hard and it might take a hand off. Too light and it won't fire."

Park nodded as we pointed the tube towards the tank, aiming as best as we could. "Fire!" Jock yelled and Park shoved that round in—just as the tank fired—*CRACK!* A shell destroyed a tree behind us, throwing wood chips all over our impromptu gun team—and our round boomed somewhere behind the tank. The mortar itself jerked itself out of our aim. "Lower!" Jock said, and we set up again.

"FIRE!" Jock screamed and Park did—a HIT! The smoke cleared down range and I saw the tank had sustained damage. The tank hatch popped and two men jumped out. I nailed one of them with a burst and dropped him; the other got behind his wounded tank and stayed put. Smart boy.

"RELOAD!" yelled Jock, and we did—and just in time. Another tank appeared and we sighted in, then fired again. Way high!

The next round went down the tube—and nothing happened!

"Misfire!" Park yelled. A spatter of gunfire went over our heads and into the trees.

"Suppressing fire!" Jock yelled, but we were already on it.

Park and Jock tipped the tube and carefully ejected the live round.

BOOM! A tank round blew up a tree behind us and I heard Ace yell.

"Ace!" I said.

"It's okay I think," he said. "Splinters in my face."

"Drag that mortar. Grab shells! We gotta move!" Jock yelled. We did, getting deeper into the woods as the tank closed on our position. The woods were a mix of clearings and copses of trees and we found a thick spot as we moved upward and hoped for the best. If they came in with more guys, we were toast.

"Crow One, this is Kilo One," Jock's radio snapped. "Relief is on the way. Sit tight. Over."

We got behind a ridge and for the next hour Park and Jock moved around and winged occasional shells over the trees and towards the field. Men attempted to gain our position and we held them off with our rifles. The woods kept the tanks from making it up, but at more than one point as I ducked machinegun fire from below I thought we were finished—and then I heard the far-off rattle of fresh gunfire and the marvelous sound of large explosions.

"Hold your fire, Crow One, friendlies incoming on your position!" I listened. The fire was done—the field was silent.

When a half-dozen Wardogs showed up at the edge of the woods escorting a medic, I finally took a deep breath. We'd secured the supplies.

But the cost!

Chapter 9

Take the Hill

I can't say I was ever close to Four-eyes. He was smart and he had no sense of humor, but his absence bothered me more than I would have thought. I missed the wet blanket. When you're part of a team for a long time, then you lose a member or two, you feel it almost like you'd miss a lost finger or something. And all of us missed Howland. He was the old-school no-nonsense soldier who reminded everyone of their dad. You couldn't help but look up to the guy. He'd saved his share of lives on the battlefield, always calm and cool. Hell, I never even heard him cuss. He was just there, getting stuff done. A mercenary's merc.

But even at the cost, we'd been lucky. Turned out there had been five tanks coming at us. We'd wrecked one, damaged another, then the boys had come in from behind and knocked out a third before the last two retreated. We'd been damned lucky there hadn't been more of them. Or worse, air support.

We waited for the trucks to come and haul the supplies back to base, then we'd been told it was time to move again.

It took us a while to find Leighton. He'd been sniped and dropped in the bushes. Never had a chance. I didn't know him well, since he'd only been in the company for a few months. He'd never cash in on his bonus now. I told myself I'd throw some roses on his grave, whenever he got a grave back Kantillon.

Three days later, I found myself walking down the edge of a well-paved highway along with most of the boys. It seems ridiculous that men are still marching in this day and age, but that's the way it goes. Never enough vehicles. And I'd lost my jeep. The other jeep had been smashed too. I decided that when I retired, I was gonna buy and ship a couple of those to the mansion I'd build out in the boondocks somewhere. I'd have a golf course, too. And I'd drive my hoverjeep around on it. And down to my rifle range. And then on to the strip of perfect beach on the edge of my property, where the local swimsuit models would do their daily photoshoots. Of course, half of them would be topless, you know, and the golden light of the setting sun reflecting off their tanned bodies, and they'd all call me Big Tommy and–

"Yo, Tommy," said Jock, interrupting my very important thoughts.

"Yeah?" I said, snapping back to the dreary reality of a long march.

"About 50km left to Corwis."

"Great," I said. "We could drive that in 20 minutes, if we had a jeep."

"If wishes were horses, then bears would be Catholic."

"I don't think that's how it goes, Sarge."

"You just don't recognize education when you hear it, Corporal."

The colonel had ordered the whole outfit on the move even though he seemed to have smoothed things out with our unhappy allies. Some of the Ulimbese stayed behind to hold the area, but the rest of them were advancing on the Corwistalian capital. For what we didn't know for sure, but rumors were that we were going to be assisting the local political process through non-electoral means. Some Ulimbese units were moving north as well, but our groups kept to themselves.

I missed the hotel, but the quicker we could get done whatever we were supposed to get done and get the heck out of here, the happier I'd be. This whole thing had been a clusterfrag from the beginning.

"So," I said, "you hear anything else on our mission?"

"Just the same-old same-old. We're probably going to take out one guy and put in some other guy who will do whatever the big intergalactic corporations want him to do."

"And the Ulimbese get what out of this?"

"Beats me," Jock said. "Maybe they get to keep what they're taking."

I looked around at the rolling countryside and brown grass. We passed a few houses here and there and occasionally some kids would watch us over hedges. It was colder up here and there had obviously been some frosts, as the dead grass evinced.

It wasn't anything I'd care about. Maybe the Ulimbese were short on farmland. Or maybe they just wanted a bigger slice of the globe.

Occasionally we'd be passed by trucks full of rocks. There was some mining operation around here. I thought back to the freighter. Mining equipment and rifles. Hmm.

"Look," I said, "if the Ulimbese are taking the capital but we're helping replace the ruler, will he be their puppet? Or will they want to keep the place for themselves and say hell with our plan? Or–"

"You sound like Four-eyes," Jock said.

He was right. I did. So I shut up. Whatever the larger plan was, it didn't matter to us. We had a job to do, and we were going to do it.

We stopped for our hourly break and I sat on the curb beneath what I assumed was a speed limit sign. I took a sip from my canteen and did some math. At the current rate, we'd get there tomorrow morning. You might think it was stupid to take a ten minute break every hour, but when you're carrying a rifle and a pack, it works a lot better than pushing until you're burnt out, then taking a long break. Little bites of break left you refreshed, like eating small amounts of food is better than starving all day before eating like a python.

So far, the ground we were covering was occupied by the Ulimbese. We passed their checkpoints now and again and they stood aside as we passed. Occasionally, some crazy Corwistalian would disrupt our column. At one point a big truck came barreling into the line ahead but no one was hurt except the driver. He unfortunately died of what we call "spurting sieve" syndrome. Very sad.

My back was feeling pretty decent. A medic had worked on it with some sort of weird chiropractic treatment and other than the bruising, I wasn't feeling quite so crimped. It actually felt pretty good to march.

The next morning we were on the outskirts of Corwis, the capital of the whole royal shebang. This was going to be the Melliol operation all over again, I figured. We'd go in, drone the artillery, shell the palace, then get the King. Though he might not want to surrender after what happened to his boy. Ah well—not my problem.

The Ulimbese had a camp set up already and we took the better part of a day claiming a farm for our own camp site. It was a good-sized commercial place with greenhouses and outbuildings, multiple sets of lodging for the employees, plus a great big plantation house the brass took for themselves as a command center. As for us grunts, we mostly set up in tents.

I slept like a rock until a mortar hit the pumphouse.

The shockwave woke me up as much as the sound did. You feel an explosion like that. You can tell the difference between a truck backfiring and a bomb exploding by waiting a second for the vibration of the air to sweep past you. That's what woke me up—*THUMP*—and then the compression rolling through me. I jumped up, catching my head on the bar of the tent over my head, grabbed my kit, and was out the door. The adrenaline coursing through my veins was like a shot of espresso injected into my neck. The other seven guys in the tent were up too and heading cautiously into the yard. Shouts and the chatter of gunfire came from outside. I reached the flap and saw multiple men racing over the hedge at one end of the yard towards a smoking farm truck. I spun around and saw a stream of water shooting into the air from the ruined remains of the farm's well. There went our fresh water.

"It's over," said Jones, slapping me on the shoulder. I jumped when he did. I was half asleep and pumped up on adrenaline at the same time.

"They took a potshot at us."

Jones had been on watch, I remembered.

"Two soldiers a few farms over" he continued. "They already got 'em. Should never have gotten this close."

"I'd say not," I said. No matter how low the tech level, you can get killed just as easily with a brick as with a disrupter.

Other than the crazy wake-up call, the rest of the day was a waiting game while Colonel Emerson worked out his plan for taking Corwis. I took full advantage of my leisure time, walking around the farm, shooting the breeze with the other guys, getting some reading in. I even took a nap in the afternoon. Some local plumbers were pressed into service to fix the well, so we had running water again by the afternoon, and a re-built pumphouse. No lie. You can get stuff done quick when you have enough guys and powerful friends. Try getting that sort of thing done at home and it would take you a week or two, at the fastest. The farmer would be happy if he ever got his place back. The new one looked better than the old one.

In the late afternoon the colonel called our squad to the house. Guys had been going in and out for meetings the entire day. Now it was our turn.

The house was a nice place with two floors and sweeping staircases leading to a second story. All wood inside, with floors that looked like they'd seen a century of use; rich, brown and smooth with age. We were called into a greatroom to the back which looked like it probably hosted country dances in happier times. Tall windows were covered with thick drapes and old rifles and landscape paintings hung on the walls. In one corner was a pile of large striped winter squash with a red ribbon on one of them. They were obviously proud of their produce.

The brass had taken a couple of tables and turned them into a staging area for the taking of Corwistal. A large map was on the table and various positions were marked with plastic figurines denoting various forces. It was a far cry from the 3-D holographic projections we usually used. I kind of liked it though. It was wholesome, you know?

The colonel was flanked by the lieutenant colonel and a couple of lieutenants, plus our coffee-stealing major.

"Good afternoon, men," he said as Jones, Park, Ward, Jock and I stood at attention. "At ease."

We relaxed and he beckoned us over to the map.

"Good job securing that supply drop. It was ugly, but you held the location against the odds and made it back."

"Thank you, sir," we responded.

"We've got another job for you now, which hopefully will run much smoother than the previous mission. Lieutenant Evans?"

The lieutenant nodded and stepped forward to the map.

"Sir! As you can see here," he gestured at the map, "we are currently located closest to the southern end of the capital. The capital itself is located next to the Ildris River, which enters the city bounds from the northeast and takes a snake-like series of up and down loops towards the south through the valley before exiting the municipality again towards the northwest. The Royal Palace is located on a hill of about 25 meters elevation over the river, on the north side of the river, in a relatively open area with only two guarded highway access points.

"In between us and the palace from our current location is a series of suburbs and an industrial district right along the river, containing warehouses, manufacturing and shipping facilities. To the northeast is the business district, with a large area of skyscrapers and–"

"Lieutenant, TMI," the colonel said, clearing his throat. "Objective, please."

"Yes sir, sorry sir."

The lieutenant pointed to a hill a solid 15 kilometers outside of the city.

"As you can see, this hill is bordered by a road to the east—which is the main artery into the capital from the south—and Lake Ildris to the west—a major water supply for Corwis—but the hill itself is mostly open. The little grey and white squares you see here and there across the top are grave markers.

"We have designated this Hill 621, though locals call it Cemetery Hill. Used to be a burial site hundreds of years ago for a nearby mining town, which has now fallen into decay. Now it's occupied by the Corwistalian Royal Regulars. We attempted a drone flyover but the drone was destroyed. We're not sure how many men are up there, but Ulimbese scouts have said there is a gun battery located there, overlooking the road.

"The reason this hill is tactically important is because it's one of the highest locations in the area and a perfect location for us to place our own guns, putting us well within howitzer range of the city itself and giving us an excellent angle for shelling anything from the port district to the royal palace."

"Thank you, Lieutenant," Colonel Emerson said. "Now, Sergeant Hanley, we need you to take a small scout team and get us locked on target so we can shell the hell out of that position."

"Yes sir," Jock said, leaning over the map. "We'll need to find a good location high enough to get us a view over Hill 621 where we can call in fire. The neighboring grid to the east, here, there's a higher spot, about two and a half kilometers out. Looks like a ridge."

"That's correct," the lieutenant chimed in. "The road itself is in a lower area between the ridge to the west and the hill to the east."

"Can we take in a vehicle?" Jock asked.

"Yes," said the lieutenant. "You can get to within about five kilometers of the hill by following the road until it reaches this bend. That area is mostly logging land, low visibility and they won't see you coming in until you come out here," he pointed on the map. "On the western side of the road it looks like forest on this map but it isn't anymore, according to scouts. This area has been clearcut and replanted within the last couple of years. New trees are only a couple of feet tall, so you'd be sitting ducks for the battery up top."

"And the other side?" Jock asked, pointing to the eastern side, which also looked to be cloaked in forest.

"Also clearcut," the lieutenant said, "but only for perhaps a half-kilometer off the road up the ridge. Back side of the ridge is a different piece of land, still wooded and sloping down to a seasonal creek bed on the other side."

"So, we get dropped off, then we can cut across, stay low through the young trees, get to the back of the ridge, then work our way to the top a few kilometers down, then sight in on the hill and call in artillery," Jock said. "No problem."

"Excellent," Colonel Emerson said. "Get ready. We need you there tonight. If you can be ready within the hour, we'll get you to your drop-off point by sundown. Take two men, Sergeant. This needs to be small, fast, and quiet. Do not allow your squad to be compromised. Do not engage the enemy unless absolutely necessary."

"Yes sir," we said with a salute. The colonel saluted in return. "Good luck, men. Take that hill and we take the town. Dismissed."

Outside, Jock looked us over.

"Falkland and Park, you're coming with me."

"Aw, c'mon Sarge!" Jones said. "What about me?"

"You stay here and braid Ward's hair for him."

"That could take a while," Ward said, running his hand over his shaved head.

"Sit tight, Jones, you'll get your chance. Both these guys have more recon experience, plus Park is certified to one-kay range."

They nodded and retreated, while Jock, Park and I hit up the supply officer. Jock got a rifle with a grenade launcher, Park took his sniper rifle along with some frag grenades and Jock gave me a heavy machine gun with a bipod, just in case we got stuck. Each of us carried two boxes of extra belts for the machinegun plus our regular packs. We also got long underwear and jacket liners. Weather would be near freezing overnight. Jock gave me the radio, reporting directly to the master gun chief. Codename "Fox".

We rode in the back of an armored vehicle, painted a flat green.

"What's up with all the boxes stuck on the side of this thing?" Park asked the Ulimbese driver.

"You never saw that before?" he said incredulously.

"No," Park said.

"Reactive armor," the driver said. "We get hit, it blows up."

"What?" I said. "This thing is a death trap!"

Jock laughed and shook his head. "Naw, I'm guessing it blows outwards."

"You got it," said the driver. "We take a hit, it triggers the box to blow, exploding outward and hopefully taking out the incoming. Controlled explosion."

The Ulimbese gunner nodded. "Yeah, it's good stuff. I've thought about putting it on my house."

"Bad neighborhood?" I asked.

"Naw. I live near a golf course, though. Fore—POW!"

"Geez," Jock said.

We arrived at our drop-off point a little before sundown and waved goodbye to our escort, then travelled out of sight of the road into the woods.

The shadows stretched long and dark across the road as Park and Jock looked over the map. We had it on a tablet and a paper version that unfolded. They stretched the latter over a rock.

"You know," Jock said, "I think we could just go straight over and down to the creek bed and hike that through, unless it's full."

"Shouldn't be," Park said. "This is the dry season."

"Great," said Jock. "Faster to take the open creek bed than try to blaze a trail through woods all the way, especially in the dark. What do you think, Tommy."

"Fine by me," I said. "Unless enemy thinks the same thing. Easy for us is easy for them."

"I'll take point," Park said.

"Agreed," said Jock, "you're sneakier than Falkland."

The temperature was dropping as the sun disappeared. Birds were settling in above with occasional squawks and peeps over whatever branch they were claiming for the evening. Overall, it was a beautiful winter evening.

"Okay," Jock said as the light faded to grey-blue. "Goggles on, let's move."

We switched to night vision and walked quietly back to the road, staying a few meters apart from each other. Line of sight was easy with thermals—none of us were going to get lost. Park held up his hand at the roadside, looked for traffic, then ran across, keeping low, into the woods on the other side. We followed, then turned northeast to find the creek bed. After a short time of moving through perfectly planted rows of pine we hit the clearcut portion. Though we couldn't see anyone out there, the chances of discovery would be too high so we stuck to the woods until we hit the creek bed another 100 meters or so in.

"Follow this up and we should find a good place to go up the ridge side," Park said. "Hopefully it's not too steep."

"Shouldn't be," Jock said, looking at the dim light of his tablet.

"We'll see," said Park and pressed forward.

The creek bed was rocky but mostly flat. There was a small trickle of water winding about in the bottom but it barely passed the sole of a boot. The full creek was a few meters across with trees stretching overhead on both sides, most of which were devoid of leaves. We'd left the pine farm behind. Tufts of dead grass grew here and there in the creek bed and dead clumps of frozen plants rustled as we passed.

We hiked along for about a kilometer, then Park waved us down and we hit the ground.

I crawled up to his position, as did Jock.

"What is it?" Jock whispered.

"Two signatures," Park said. "Farther down the creek bed where it starts to turn. 100 meters. They didn't spot us, so far as I could tell."

"They must have night vision or they wouldn't be out here." I said.

"Yes," Jock said. "Not as good as ours, but they have it."

"Soldiers?" I said.

"Probably," said Park.

"Alright, let's get cover. We'll ambush 'em. Tommy—get in the woods on the left. Park, find a sniping position."

"Roger," I said and crept up the bank and took a position behind the almost horizontal trunk of an ancient tree sprawling over the creek bed and got my machine gun ready. The last thing I wanted to do was fire it up and alert all Ulixis to our presence, but if we needed it, we needed it.

I could see them now. Two soldiers, as their walk and rifles attested.

Park had a silencer on his rifle but it was still going to be louder than we'd like. Jock had taken a position behind a boulder on the other side of the creek bed. And we waited.

The men walked closer, almost at a leisurely pace. I had been right about the creek bed being too easy.

The seconds ticked by, then I saw Jock raise his hand. The lead man was only 20 meters from his position, the second guy about 5 meters behind him.

At 15 meters he dropped his hand and there was a bark from my right. The rear man fell with a grunt and the lead soldier hit the ground. Another bark from Park's rifle and he jerked, then lay still.

I saw Park slink down from the trees. "All clear," he said quietly and we moved towards the bodies.

First guy through the chest, second through the skull. Both very dead. Park took off the night vision goggles of the trailing man and tried them on.

"Lousy," he said. "No wonder we got the drop on them."

"Good thing," Jock said. "I'm going to bet that's the only patrol we'll run into on this route."

Park put his own goggles back on and tossed the enemy's to the ground, then snapped pictures of both their faces for later ID by the intel guys.

I retracted the bipod on my gun and we all got back into position and kept moving.

Everything was quiet for another kilometer until suddenly Park held his hand up again. We waited for a minute, then another, and then, suddenly, multiple thermal signatures flashed in front of us, racing across the creek bed. I almost opened up before realizing it was a herd of some kind of animal.

Jock swore and shook his head. "I did not expect that."

I heard Park chuckle. "Too bad it wasn't a different time. I can cook a mean venison steak."

We took the interruption for another look at the map.

"A little farther," Jock said, "then we can move up."

"No," Park said, "we need to cut up now."

I looked up the side of the ridge. It wasn't terribly steep, though the creek bed at this point was heading downwards at more of a slope. The banks were getting higher. Another hundred meters and it would be like cutting through a canyon.

Jock looked down. "Fine, Park. Let's hope the woods aren't too thick."

We went up through the woods. They were thickest by the creek itself but thinned somewhat as we moved up. We followed a diagonal, moving along and up towards our objective. As we neared the ridgetop, the growth got thicker and thornier on the thinner soil and going was slow. We finally broke through and onto the scrubby top of the ridge at around 22:30. Park went low when we reached the top, in case the enemy had optics on the site. We followed suit.

The location commanded an excellent view of the surrounding countryside. I made out the course of the road and the clearcut area of trees, then off and up the other hill. Even at night through my goggles I could see scattered gravestones mixed with shrubs and trees, then up top an enemy encampment. It looks like they chose some sort of hilltop park area for their operations, unless they'd cleared it themselves. There was a winding paved road up to the location which we could glimpse in patches through the tree cover.

"Tommy," Park said, "I'll give you info—relay to base."

"You got it," I said, keying in my radio. "Base, this is Fox. Prepare to receive data on enemy position."

Park looked through his binoculars.

"Three squadrons of armor," he said.

"A gun battery—8 guns. 100+ millimeter, I would say…"

"Eight armored troop transports…"

"And looks like about a company of regulars."

I repeated each line after him. "What's the ETA on enemy position data, Fox?"

"Give me a few," Park said and I dutifully repeated.

Retrieving the paper map, a minute later we'd worked out where the enemy position was on the grid.

"Dammit," Jock said, "I'd trade my pinky toe for GPS right about now."

"Yeah," said Park as he eyed up his thumb against the enemy position. "Damn low tech."

"Seriously," Jock said. "That restriction is stupid. We can have advanced optics but not GPS?"

"It's the Ascendancy," I said, remembering what I'd learned on the way in. "No military satellites. They're pretty arbitrary about the tech levels."

"Sure," Park said, "We can't put our satellites up, but civvies can use GPS?"

"We should have figured out how to tap into the civilian system."

Jock snorted dismissively. "I suspect the Ascendancy would frown on that."

I watched Park look at the map, then the enemy position, then back at the map, making notes with a pencil. He was eyeing out locations, probably taking something like a tank and using it as a measuring point off the road to see how far into the grid the enemy location might be. See, when you can't use a laser, you just pick something you know the size of, then get a good guesstimate by using lengths. In this case, it wasn't all that easy because of the slope.

He pencilled down a number and gave it to me, then I called it in to artillery.

"Roger," came the voice of the gunnery sergeant. We waited...and then heard "Shot—over!"

"Shot—out!" I said and started counting. 1...2...3...4...5...6... 7...8...9..."Splash, over!" he called. Then *POW!* "Splash out!" I radioed back as a big burst of dirt and smoke from the hillside maybe 40 meters past the enemy position announced the arrival of the first barrage.

"Close," Park said. "Drop 50, left 25. Fire for effect. Over." The enemy were moving around now and more lights had come on at the base. I radioed in Park's adjustments and they were acknowledged by the gunnery sergeant. A few moments later,

"Shot, over!"

"Shot, out!"

1...2...3...4...5...6...7...8...9...

"Splash over!"

RATTLE THUMP-THUMP-THUMP RATTLE the rounds crashed in!

"Splash out!" I yelled back.

This time the barrage was in front of the enemy position by about 10 meters. Park gave me another number and I sent it in—and we really nailed 'em! We took a chunk out of the road to the east that time, and it was good timing as a tank column was just starting to move.

Park was boxing them in. We did this for over an hour, moving in and out and towards the center until the base was ruined and most of the men had fled. A few vehicles got away, but the battery was destroyed and a lot of guys weren't going home again.

"Enemy position destroyed," I reported to the gunny. Now we'd watch as our boys came in.

Along the road from the south Wardogs and Ulimbese marched and rolled in, approaching the hill, then heading up along the sides. We could see muzzle flashes and grenade bursts, but it didn't take long. Within a half hour of the operation's launch from the highway, it was over. Hill 621 was ours without a single casualty.

We taken out the transports, four tanks, the gun battery, plus I found out later that our guys took 200 prisoners, were all ID'd before being paroled with a warning that if they were taken prisoner again, they'd be immediately shot.

Don't ever let people tell you mercenaries ain't smart. We've usually got the best intel because we're professional enough to pay for it.

Chapter 10

Bring the Noise

Within a day, we'd fixed the road and moved four howitzers to the top of Cemetery Hill. Two days later, Kilo Company was up top watching the Ulimbese siege of Corwis begin.

Two divisions of Imperial troops had blocked off all entrances and exit routes from the city and spread patrols across the country side. If you were in, you were in. If out, you were out. There must have been some panic in the city, too, and some mob activity because I saw multiple fires and columns of smoke rising on the first day of the siege—and that was before we started shelling.

The shelling began early the second day. The almost unbearable noise of the howitzers required all of us to wear ear protection while they were in operation.

At this point most of us were just watching and waiting. During a break in the shelling, Park and I walked the row of howitzers together and I was pleased to spot our lucky gun.

"There," I said, "that's our gun," pointing it out to Park.

"How do you know?" he said.

"Look at the paint on the back tripod. See the white? From ramming the side of the shipping container."

"How about that?" he said, affectionately patting the barrel. "Good gun. Nice gun."

"You know, if Four-eyes were here he'd remind you that's not a gun. It's a howitzer."

"Yeah," Park said. "Aspie bastard. I miss him."

We looked down towards the city for a few moments in silence, then Park turned back and looked at the gun with a strange expression.

"Nukes," he muttered.

"What?" I said.

"Nuke shells. For these guns. Why do you think we had nuke shells?"

"I dunno," I said, "but it makes no damn sense for us to have nukes when we can't even have GPS."

"Yes," he said. "I would think it would be illegal."

"What's illegal?" said Ward, walking up behind us.

"Your ass," said Park.

Ward ignored him.

"We were talking about the shells Jock found during the cargo drop," I said. "They're probably illegal."

"Under the tech laws?" Ward said. "Ulixis has nuclear power plants, so nuclear weapons are not out of the question. But if I'm wrong, we could get in huge trouble."

"Yeah," I said, "but the colonel must know what he's doing."

"He does," said Park. "They must not be illegal under Ascendancy law. He may have steel in his spine but he's no dummy.

"If they're legal here, why wouldn't the Corwistalians or Ulimbese have nuked each other yet?" Ward said. "I mean, if you killed my kid, I'd burn your country to glowing cinders for the next 1000 years."

"You have a kid?" I said.

"Yeah," said Ward. "He's two."

Park grunted and shook his head.

"Perhaps they're illegal locally," I ventured. "Some planetary treaty."

"Makes sense to me," Park said. "And the colonel wouldn't give a rat's ass about that, provided we were paid well enough."

Suddenly we were surrounded by a howitzer crew. "Why the hell are you dipwads touching my gun?" said the angry gunnery sergeant.

"She was coming on to me," Park said as we backed hastily away.

The gunny shook his head, unamused. Gun crews love their guns. He probably have been less touchy if we'd felt up his wife in front of him. We got out of the way quickly. Jock showed up, hair wet and buttoning his jacket, apparently having taken a shower at one of the field showers that had been set up for us.

"Ulimbese armored column coming in, boys," he said. "Just heard they busted through our previous location and are heading in from the south."

Two of our howitzers were now facing south and the boys were digging in the spades.

Then it was done and they were loaded, fired, then were reloaded and fired again and again. I wasn't sure how far out this column was but I hoped they were pinning it down before I ended up sent down to the road with an RPG.

"We flying a drone this time?" I yelled to Jock in between volleys. He shrugged, but Park yelled back at me. "Enemy has good anti-air capabilities. We've got to save the few we have left. Only for emergencies at this point. Gotta wait for our actual supply drop to arrive."

"If it arrives," Jock said. "I'm starting to think we're like Robinson Crusoe out here, stuck scrounging off the land until we get picked up again."

"Who was he?" Ward asked.

"It's literature. You wouldn't understand."

Park snickered and Ward rolled his eyes. Everyone knew Jock wasn't much of a reader.

As for the Corwistalian relief operation, the enemy armored column never made it to our position. We punched holes in them until they turned tail, then we pounded the rest of their armor into scrap.

The choice of Cemetery Hill was a good one. We approved. The colonel always seemed to know what he was doing.

That evening the howitzers resumed their sporadic shelling of the city, though I felt they could have hit a lot harder if they wanted to.

From what I could tell, they weren't even aiming at the palace. I didn't find out why until later.

It turned out they were waiting until a certain VIP member of the royal family got out of the city. And guess which platoon got tapped to go in and get him?

The bastards.

Chapter 11

In and Out

The crowds were thin as we walked into the restaurant. It was a nice place.

"Don't pick at your makeup," Jock hissed at Park. All of us were dolled up in civvies. Getting into the city had been a piece of cake thanks to a few of Royal Cousin Beauregard's men. We hiked to the edge of the woods, changed into civvies, then a taxi picked us up, driven by one of his guys. The checkpoint waved us through and then we were dropped off in town. Easy. The makeup did feel weird, though. All three of us had various cuts and bruises from combat and three guys who looked like they'd been brawling would attract suspicion, so a corporal with stage makeup experience gave us a touch-up. Weird, I know. It was a big deal to be chosen—we were going to make bank. Jock, Park and I had really shone in taking Cemetery Hill, so we were thrown right back in. I itched to have a rifle or at least a couple of grenades but this mission wouldn't allow for that. Corwis didn't really have a gun culture like some worlds. Sad. Instead, each of us had a concealed pistol and a knife. We also had stunpens. They were simple—looked like a little pen, had multiple doses of a fast-acting knockout drug in it. Thump it into someone and they were out like a light. Bad thing was you had to be close to use it. I had to keep myself from patting my gun now and again, I felt so naked walking around in civvies.

The maître d' approached and bowed slightly. "Good evening, gentlemen. Do you have a reservation?"

"Yes," Jock replied. "Arnette."

I could smell steak and fried potatoes and my mouth was watering. It would be a heck of a lot better than camp food. I'd almost do this mission for free if they threw in a tankard of bitter and some ice cream for dessert.

The maître d' checked his tablet and frowned.

"I'm sorry, sir. It appears your reservation is not on here."

"It's not under my name," Jock said. "Arnette was the gentleman we were supposed to meet."

"No, it doesn't appear to be in the system at all. We do have a table, however, if you would like one for your party."

"No, thank you," Jock replied, much to the dissatisfaction of my growling stomach. I knew steak wasn't important to the plan, but hey, I wasn't going to turn it down on purpose. Of course, we had bigger problems than steak now. If we'd been compromised, we were in big trouble.

Arnette was supposed to be Prince Beauregard's alias of the evening. He needed to get out of the city safely and we were his escorts back to camp. Word was that he'd be replacing the king once we were through. That explained the half-hearted shelling of the city. We weren't going to pound it until the guy was safely out. As soon as we got out of the city with the Royal Cousin they'd probably unleash hell.

We stepped back into the street behind Jock, acting as casually as we could. "Come on," he said, "let's get to a less crowded spot and work this out."

A few moments later we were leaning against a wall on a nicely-tiled walkway between two buildings as if waiting for dates to show up. Captain Marks had told us to slouch before sending us off. "Posture is a dead giveaway," he said. "We can't do anything about your obvious fitness level, but just look at civilian guys and act like them. And don't start fraternizing with the local girls."

Easier said than done, I thought, as a buxom brunette in a red dress and a white scarf bobbed past me and looked me over. Hey, some guys just have it.

Jock was on his comm. It looked like a regular phone but radioed directly back to base. He frowned as he read a message.

"Change of plans," he said. "Something went wrong."

"Yeah, I figured that out when you turned down dinner," I said.

"Worse than that," he said. "We've got no sign of our contact at all. He's either compromised or he's hiding."

"Great," Park said. "So what now?"

Jock dialed a number and held up a finger. A short, whispered conversation ensued, then he hung up and dialed another number. After a minute, he ended the call and turned back to us.

"First, the prince's men say Beauregard was picked up by a few heavies and hasn't been seen since."

That didn't sound good. "So we're out of here?" I said.

"Negative on that," Jock said. "Seems we have eyes on the other prince, the new heir. We're going to bring him in instead."

"For what?" Park said.

"He's a hell of a bargaining chip, and we're not far from his location now."

"Where's that?" I said.

"Planet Spice," Jock said with a grin.

"It's gotta be a whorehouse," I said.

Jock nodded happily.

"Great," I said, "and me without my booster shots." Ace was going to be pissed he missed this mission.

"We're about twelve blocks from it," Jock said quietly, looking at his phone. "The prince has three guards we'll have to take out. We'll go in, see if we can get a room next to his, then blow through through the wall and take him. Follow my lead and act natural. We're just healthy young men out on the town. Now let's roll."

We stepped out of the alley and started walking west towards the whorehouse.

"So," said Jock brightly as we walked, "who's going to win the Series this year?"

"Asteroids," said Park.

"Asteroids?" I said. "They're not even in class A."

"That would explain the odds against them," admitted Park.

"Well," said Jock, "I think the new padding rules are stupid. It's a man's game, not some sort of padded low-grav gym for coddled youth."

"Agreed," I said. "The padding takes the guts out of the game."

"It's also an invitation to get hurt worse," Jock said.

"Yeah," I said. "I heard that. The players hit harder because they think they can't get hurt, right?"

"Exactly," Jock said. "Safety gear is actually worse for injuries."

"Here's the thing," Park complained. "Some of those guys get paid more for one game than we make in a whole year of missions. You know that? And they're just playing a game. Sure, they might get hurt, but ain't no one going to blow their heads off."

The district was lit brightly with strings of bulbs around small trees planted in the sidewalk, banners in windows, clothing, purses, boots, even an antique book store. In between were cafes and bars. Live music echoed from multiple establishments as we passed, washing together with the honking of horns, talking and the sound of visiscreens broadcasting sportsgames. It was obviously a night life hotspot, but the crowds were subdued and many of the open establishments had few patrons. Having your city besieged and shelled wasn't good for business.

The eight block marked the beginning of the red light district. Outlines of legs in neon tubes, darker colors and blue and purple lighting, with men in leather and women in slinky dresses in knots of conversation or smoking.

It looked like most red light districts I've seen, though I laughed involuntarily when I saw a poster in the black-painted window of one seedy looking joint. It had three topless women standing with their arms linked and their midsections blurred out. Not their breasts, their belly buttons.

"What the hell?" Park said, observing the same thing.

"It's must be a local fetish," I said. "The exposed stomach is a major turn-on here. Full navel exposure prohibited by law."

"That's crazy," Park said.

"Bellies are hot," Jock said. "There was this one chick I used to know, she had one of those belly buttons like a little slit."

I'm partial to a pierced belly myself, but I didn't feel any need to share my thoughts on the subject.

"Thanks, but we're busy," Park said, pushing away a heavily made-up woman who reached out to brush his arm as we slowed our pace. At least, I think she was a woman.

And then we were there. Planet Spice was a white brick building lit with neon purple lights along its lines. The windows were mirrors and a hefty pair of bouncers in black stood at the door, checking IDs and letting people in and out.

The big acne-scarred and stocky bald bouncer on the left held out his hand as we walked up and Jock passed him his forged ID. Park and I did the same. He looked at us, then at the IDs, then waved us in.

The other bouncer was tall and skinny, and had shining black hair pulled into a pony tail. He was carrying, too; I could just make out the tell-tale bulge in his breast pocket. I heard him click a tally counter as we passed. One guy must have been the intake, the other the outtake. Either way, we'd want to take out the guy with the weapon first.

Then we were inside. A tall woman in tights and a halter top which barely contained her well-shaped and unencumbered breasts met us with a slight smile on her red mouth. "Are you here for the show this evening or are you looking for a little more private entertainment?"

"We're meeting some friends here tonight," Jock said, nodding ahead towards a hallway to the right where three men stood rigidly. "That looks like them there."

He pulled a credit card from his wallet and handed it to the woman. She scanned its chip on a small necklace she wore, then smiled brightly at him. "Very good, gentlemen," she said, "you may go on back and you'll be taken care of."

We walked in, passing an archway which opened on a stage where a band played a strange, never resolving tune as a pair of women wound ribbons around their almost naked bodies as they danced. I was suddenly reminded how very long it had been since I last–

"Good evening," Jock said to our purported friends. They were wearing civilian clothes but given their bearing they were obviously some sort of security detail, most likely the prince's. Two of them definitely had pistols, the other one appeared to have something strapped to his back under his jacket. He'd be the gunner, was my guess.

"What would you like this evening?" said a lean blonde as she materialized from behind a curtain to our right, clad in soft, flowing silver.

"Well," said Jock, "I hadn't quite decided yet. Me and my boys just closed a big deal we've been working on for some time, and I thought you ladies might have an idea how we could celebrate it."

She smiled. "I think we just might have a few ideas. Would you like to see the drinks menu or would you prefer to choose your dates for the evening?"

"How about a few drinks?" Jock said. "Whiskey for me."

"Rhysalan Newt, if you got it," said Park, ordering a popular nutritive yeast beer.

"Whatever local brew you recommend," I said to the girl.

"Check that out," Park said to me as she swished away. He watched her until she disappeared behind the crowd. "Think she's on the menu?"

Jock tried a door but it was locked, then he tried a second one that it opened to a rich, red-carpeted room, thick with the odor of incense. He glanced inside, then shut the door. Then he moved towards the door on the next room. One of the big men quickly grabbed his arm.

"What do you think you're doing?," he growled as the other two guards moved closer.

"I'm looking for the bathroom," Jock said. The guy frowned and jerked his thumb towards the end of the hall.

"Oh, hey, thanks man," Jock said, looking relieved.

Now we knew the third door concealed the prince.

The blonde reappeared with our drinks. "And now," she said, "I'm sure you'd like to relax and see some of the girls. They're in the lounge."

"Pick some for us," Jock said, leaning in so the guards couldn't hear him, "and can we have the suite here?" He pointed to the closed door. "It was recommended to me. And my friends are a little nervous. We'll have a few drinks, then see where the night takes us."

"First time?" she said.

"Yeah," he said. "For them. They're Space Mormons. Not used to girls."

The girl laughed and patted his arm. "The suite is yours," she said, opening the door wide and waving us in. "Enjoy your drinks and I'll bring a couple of lady friends for you in a moment. Any preferences?"

"Female," Jock said.

"Of course," she giggled, then disappeared.

"Geez, Jock," I said, "you're a bastard." He grinned and shut the door behind us. The room was richly appointed. There was a large flat screen on one wall, mirrors on the ceiling, a table where an incense burner slowly smoked, making little rising rings in the air. A few sprawling ottomans and dim lamps completed the look. We looked around the room quickly. It had a private bathroom, all in black tile with both a shower and a huge tub which looked capable of fitting five people.

"Don't touch anything," said Park. "You'll catch something."

"Nah," said Jock, "they probably sterilize everything between customers. This is high-class. Not like the places you're used to."

Park snorted. Jock knelt on top of the ottoman residing by the wall between this suite and the one containing the prince, then gently tapped the wall in a few places. He grimaced and swore. "I should have figured," he said. "It's solid."

"Why would you figure?" I said.

"Noise reduction."

"Guess it would spoil the mood to hear some fat guy grunting and bellowing from the next room," I said.

"Unless you like that sort of thing," said Jock. "Okay, this ain't gonna work. I've been in apartments before where you could punch through a wall with your fist. Not here."

"Too bad," said Park. "We could still use a charge to get through, though."

"No," I said, putting my ear against the wall and knocking myself. "This is too heavy. The charge required to blow through would probably kill everyone on the other side."

"Plan B, then," Jock said. "Tommy, I want you to plan our escape route from the building. HQ sent me building diagram already." He showed me the tablet where an old tax document showed the complete layout of the brothel. "This may not be up to date, so you need to wander around first. See if you can get a girl to take you so you won't stick out."

"And then we go where, out to the alley?" I asked, pointing to the back of the building.

"Bingo," said Jock.

There was a light knock at the door and the silver-clad hostess came in, along with three other girls. All of them were slim and attractive, wearing thin clothes that revealed lots of nubile woman flesh. Two blondes and one redhead.

"Good evening," the new girls crooned with big smiles, each of them sidling expertly up to one of us. "Would you like some company?"

"Yeah," said Park, slipping an arm around the red-haired girl who had chosen him. A bleach-blonde picked me. She had glowing tattoos made her arms look like a landing strip at night, but she had fantastic breasts. Jock had a blonde with bright-blue heels that showed off her excellent legs to advantage.

"I'm Aurora," she said.

"Of course you are," I said, giving my girl a little squeeze. "So, Aurora, it's my first time here. Can you show me around?"

"What do you want to see?"

"Oh, you know, anything that would be out of the ordinary. I'm looking for something different. Something unusual."

She smiled, understanding. "Want to take a look at the Dungeon of Dreams?"

"No," I said. "So, this dungeon, is it downstairs?"

"Yeah," she said, sliding her finger down my chest. "So, have you been a bad boy, or have I been a bad girl?"

I hazarded a guess. "You look like you've been a very, very bad girl."

She shivered happily and tugged on my hand. If the dungeon was where I thought it was based on the architectural drawing, it might be a good access point to the alley. If we could nab the prince, then we'd be able to get out.

We went down a set of stairs and were passed by two sweaty red-faced men walking upwards, led up by two girls. The men averted their faces, but one of the girls winked at me.

"Did you want a menu? Aurora asked."

"Drinks?" I said.

She stuck out her tongue and handed me a sheet of squiggly writing with prices.

"I can't read," I said, and she laughed.

"No, I'm serious."

"Well, then, maybe you'd like a little time with a teacher?" she said.

"Maybe," I said as we walked into the dungeon. A black lingerie-clad woman was wiping down the seat of some machine I didn't want to think about. The place looked more like a freaky gym to me than a sex dungeon.

"So…" she said, expectantly.

"Is there an exit to the alley from in here?" I asked her.

"What?" she said, clearly surprised. "Um, yeah, actually, there is."

She indicated a door towards the left rear of the room and I nodded.

"You know, this isn't quite what I was expecting. Let's go back upstairs and get to know each other better. And I could use a drink anyhow."

She shrugged indifferently and we headed back up. The door to the room was closed so she knocked. A moment later, Jock opened the door and let us in, then closed it behind us.

Aurora gasped, then collapsed into my arms as he touched his stun-pen to her neck, then I carried her over to one of the beds that wasn't already occupied by one of the three other unconscious girls.

"Did you find an exit," said Jock.

"Yeah, down in the basement. There's a dungeon two floors down. Exit to the right rear, must lead to outside stairs that go up to the alley."

"Anything else?" Jock asked as Park screwed a silencer onto his pistol, then stuffed the pistol in his waistband.

"Easy escape route. Down the stairs, through the dungeon, then out the alley."

"I'm ready," Park said.

"Right," said Jock. "We take the three guards in the hall, bust open suite door, knock out the prince, get him down the stairs and out back. I called one our contact. He'll have a vehicle waiting in the alley."

"Easy enough," I said. "Back door is going to kick off an alarm, though. And what happens if we get caught in the hallway? People are going in and out all the time."

"We move fast," said Jock.

"We could also call in an artillery strike," Park said.

"On our heads?" I said.

He shrugged. "They've got the building on a grid already. We run, they blow the place up, no one would even know we took the prince."

"Geez, Park," Jock said, "you're a cold bastard. I like it."

Park shrugged.

The sergeant made the call, confirmed that the artillery was on standby, then stuck it back in his pocket.

"Ready?" he said. I nodded, gripping my gun in a suddenly sweaty hand. There was something else…

Jock put his hand on the doorknob. "Okay, we'll walk out and shut the door behind us, see who is in the hall, then strike as fast as possible when I give the go-ahead. Maybe we can tip off some of the girls, too."

Jock held up his hand. 3 fingers, 2, 1…and he opened the door calmly and we strolled out.

The three guards were still there, along with a girl with a tray of drinks heading to a room down the hall.

"Too quick for my liking," Jock said loudly to the men, his eye on the girl. "You know, sometimes they just start bucking and you lose it."

She opened the door, walked through, then closed it behind her.

"Now!" he said and Park neatly drew and put a hole through the guard's head, then swiveled and took out the other as I jammed my stunpen into the other. Jock kicked the door and blew it inwards on the first blow, breaking the lock but not the door. There was a scream from the inside and a shout. So much for surprise.

We jumped through to find a naked man on a bench with two naked women squirming on top of him, covered in slick oil. The women screamed but shut up fast when Park showed his gun and told them to shut their traps. They went quiet real fast and tried to cover themselves with their hands.

"What is this?" yelled the prince, as he looked up wide-eyed from the table. "How dare y–!"

Jock stabbed him in the ass with his pen and he went limp on the table.

"What about the girls?" I said.

"Girls," Jock said, "do you want to live?" The two women nodded their heads in the affirmative. "Then sit down and shut up. We don't want to hurt you, but any trouble and we'll shoot you in your pretty little heads."

Jock dialed in for a strike, telling them to give us ten minutes to get clear, and then the siren started.

"Shit," he muttered, "now we're going to have to kill some people."

As if on cue, the two bouncers we'd met out front rushed into the room with short clubs, just in time to meet me and Park with our pistols. We dropped them; one of the girls started to scream, but her friend quickly hushed her.

"Help me grab the prince," Jock said, "Park, cover us."

I grabbed the prince but could barely hold him he was covered in so much oil. "Dammit!" I said. "It's like grabbing an eel!" as he slipped onto the floor out of my grasp.

"Towel him off," Jock said, and threw a towel at me. The two of us rubbed some of the oil off and tried again, getting a much better grip this time. Then another girl showed up at the door, and Park yanked her in, putting his hand over her mouth and his gun to her head.

"Listen, ladies," said Jock to her and the other two girls, "You are in serious danger. Everyone is! Get a few girls and have them drag out the four unconscious women in the next room, then tell all the other girls to get the hell out of the building. Get at least a block away. There is a bomb in it and it's going to explode in ten minutes. Go now. If you stay here, all of you will die."

They nodded obediently and ran into our old room.

We ran into the hallway, hauling the prince between us. Mustache guy opened the door to the stairs and we headed down to the dungeon. There we ran into two more girls who screamed as we hauled the body past. I didn't see the door right away, thanks to all the curtains and equipment and shit at the back of the room, plus it was dark—and then I saw an exit light and we hit the crashbar to get into the alley. *CRACK!* A blast of shotgun pellets slammed into the door as we went through and I felt a sting of pain in my right ear. I ducked to the ground, dropping the prince's legs and saw a fat old guy with a thick mustache screaming at us and brandishing a shotgun. I yanked my gun out of my waist but Park was faster, jumping back in and hitting the guy three times in center mass.

Then the girls inside really screamed but I ignored them as we made it out to the alley. I heard sirens approaching.

"Where's our car?" Jock hissed into his radio.

The sirens got louder and I saw the lights of approaching emergency vehicles. A car appeared at the end of the alley, lights flashing, then three more behind him.

"The police," the guard gasped. "They'll shoot to kill."

I heard the sound of chopper blades. Holy Possenti, they'd called out everyone.

"Over the wall!" Jock yelled at us, and we hauled the prince's limp body over the wall at the back of the alley. I saw a few of the whores jumping the wall as well but they sure weren't following us. Behind the brothel was an apartment complex and we ran down into it across the parking lot as fast as we could while carrying a limp body. The police lit their lamps and started sweeping. The light found and followed us.

"You!" boomed a voice over a megaphone. "Drop the body!"

"5," Jock said, setting down his side of the prince as I released mine. "4..."

"Hands up!" a cop boomed over the fence. "We see you!"

"2..." Jock said, calmly raising his arms as we did the same. "1..."

I heard the whistle of incoming fire for a second, then the brothel exploded in flames, debris and dust. Again and again the shells came in, knocking the walls over onto the police cars as smoke poured upwards.

"Grab him!" said Jock. "Run!"

We ran through the parking lot and got around front, where I tripped over a stone statuette that looked like a weasel, half-dropping the prince.

"Careful," said Jock, "this guy's worth more than we are."

A few moments later a sleek black SUV appeared and picked us up.

"Where the hell were you?" Jock demanded of the driver.

"I had to leave the alley, sir. I was told to."

"By who?" he asked.

"Fire chief, sir."

"Fire chief?" Jock sputtered. "The goddam FIRE CHIEF told you to move?"

"He said it was a hazard, sir," the driver said sheepishly.

I looked out the window at the flames licking the sky and laughed out loud.

"Listen," Jock said as we jumped in, "you'll need to haul it. Do you have any more men coming?"

"Yes, there are four more cars of men down the block. They'll follow."

The driver pulled onto the road and down a few blocks, then looped around. As he did, the other cars followed. Behind us, a helicopter circled over the flaming building. I heard the sounds of sirens and yelling. Traffic was out of control, but fortunately it was mostly in the other direction.

We picked up the highway without trouble and I thought we were in for smooth sailing. Jock called in and gave our position as I looked out at the lights of the city. I wondered if the hookers had all gotten out. Probably not. Life sucked. Then you died in a howitzer barrage.

"Sir…" said the driver suddenly. "Up ahead…"

The vehicle slowed. Up ahead the road must have been blocked, as I saw an angry red sea of taillights.

"Pull over!" said Jock. "We need another route!" The man did, and our escort followed.

"Plan B," said Jock, keying in his phone tablet. "Kite Crew, this is Scotsman, I need an eye in the sky. Track my signal."

"Negative, Scotsman," came a voice over the phone. "Surveillance over the city has been disallowed, over."

"Countermand that order," came another voice. "This is Kilo One. You will provide support to Scotsman."

"Roger that, Kilo One. We will have eye in sky in five."

"I need to know how we can get out of here fast," Jock said. "Get me a clear route. Main highway is blocked. Over."

"Roger," said Kite Crew, "we read you. Routes incoming, over."

My heart thumped. Waiting by the road was worse than fighting. I hated sitting, and it wasn't like a convoy of five black vehicles wasn't suspicious. It was suspicious as hell.

The minutes crept by. Then Jock's tablet dinged softly. A map was up, showing alternate routes and enemy units.

"There," Jock said, showing the driver, "take us through there!"

The driver gunned the engine into an illegal turn in the middle of the highway and back the way we'd come. He cut over onto a side road through an industrial district and I caught a glimpse of the river through the warehouses, the city lights gently reflecting in its lapping waves.

We got a ways down the road, which ran roughly parallel to the main highway for a stretch, then dipped lower as the highway raised away in a wall of concrete. The industrial area was mostly dead, though a couple of guys smoking next to a truck watched with questioning looks as we passed. Probably wondering what an official motorcade was doing down by the docks.

"Scotsman, this is Kite Crew," Jock's radio crackled. "We've got incoming behind you. Five vehicles. Almost certainly military."

I looked back and saw headlights coming down the curve off the highway way behind us.

"Roger," Jock responded. "Go faster," he told the driver.

"Looks like the police handed things over," Park muttered.

The driver gunned it under a tall highway bridge, big pillars of concrete covered with graffiti near ground level. To our left were warehouses and industrial shops, and behind them I could glimpse a tall concrete wall.

And then we heard the hoot of a train whistle.

"Scotsman, this is Kite Crew. We have a train incoming on your position, over."

"Great, thanks," Jock said, "I hear it now. Will we be boxed in?"

"Possibly," came the voice. "We cannot see you at this moment. And yes—there you are. Don't think you'll make it to the rails before the train. Over."

"Roger," said Jock, then cursed.

Behind us, the lights approached.

And then we saw the light of the train coming from the right.

"Speed up," Park said.

"No way," said the driver, "we can't make it!"

He slowed, and the train passed in front of us, painfully slow, car after car. Clack-clunk-clack-clunk-clack-clunk—and the lights were nearing from behind.

Then the train stopped.

"Shit," Jock said, "we're stuck."

"What do we do!?" the driver said, "if they catch us with the prince we're dead!"

"I hope you can swim," Jock said grimly. "Kite Crew, send in a missile. Target the sea wall, 100 meters east of our position. Right now!"

"Roger, that. Fire incoming."

There was a whistle, then a spectacular boom as a large chunk of the wall was destroyed.

"Run to the hole! Now!" yelled Jock and we grabbed the prince and hauled him from the vehicle.

The popping of automatic fire came from the vehicles behind us as we ran to the wall and climbed through the rubble. On the other side was a flat strip of concrete walk along the wall, running along the riverside. Here and there steps led down to docks and moorings.

"Park—cover our retreat," Jock yelled as we moved along the walk. Park clicked delay timers on two grenades and tossed them back towards the entrance, then fell in behind our rebel allies, checking our six regularly. A moment later, a group of four or five guys came through the wall, just in time for his frags to burst, smashing them to the ground, probably in pieces. That would keep them back for a bit.

"More men are coming," the driver said, "though I don't know if they can get us out from here."

"We need a boat," I said to Jock, getting really tired of carrying the prince.

"Scotsman this is Kite Crew," the radio interrupted. "The drone is down, repeat, drone is down, over."

"Roger," said Jock, then turned to us. "No more eye in the sky."

"What about those boats?" Park said, gesturing towards the vessels in the river.

"No way," said Jock. "You ever see the controls on one of those big ones? We couldn't operate one if we tried. By the time we figured out how to start the engines—if we figured it out—they'd hit us with an RPG."

We kept moving along the wall and the terrain changed from industrial to country as we got farther out of town.

And then the wall ended and we were looking out at countryside. I could make out the highway in the distance.

"We could pick up the road," Park said, as we continued walking along the river. "Looks clearer here. Probably only a few kilometers back to the front."

TAK-TAK-TAK!

The sound of gunfire came from behind us. More men were approaching—we saw headlights that may have been trucks or jeeps, followed by the strobing lights of police cars. Reinforcements!

"Then again," said Park as we moved as fast as we could along the river's edge, "maybe we'll just stick to the water."

"I got one better," Jock said, pointing down to a log cabin building about 500 meters ahead of us. Canoes were stacked along the side of the building in tall racks and there was a sign featuring smiling men and women and children in canoes.

"Perfect," I said. "They'll shoot us from the riverbank."

"Better than staying put," Jock said. "Listen, we'll secure that building and start getting canoes in the water. Shoot back and pin down the incoming. Park—you're the FO—take the radio and call in artillery."

"We're pretty damn close," Park said.

"Don't screw up," Jock grunted. Park nodded and called in.

The rebels took took positions around the building, sending fire back towards the incoming enemy. The enemy had been forced to stop their vehicles and come down the hillside towards us, making them good targets. I wished for a rifle. And then *THUMPTHUMP-THUMP!* the first set of rounds came in, mostly behind the enemy.

"Better than on top of us," Park muttered, quickly recalculating as he dialed in another strike. "Drop 100—fire for effect!"

As he did his thing, we were throwing canoes in the water.

Bullets hit around us as we shoved off, but the artillery shells flew in, keeping back the enemy. Then I saw a tank crest the hill.

"Shit!" I yelled. "Haul it! Haul it!" The rebels had seen the tank too and were racing to jump into canoes as the invigorated enemy kept firing despite the incoming artillery. A bullet went right through both walls of the canoe in between Jock and I as we paddled and we raced forward like madmen, throwing water and getting into the center of the stream, tugging until our hearts felt like they'd burst.

THUMP-CRACK! A tree exploded on the riverbank in front of us as a tank round nailed its trunk. We pushed harder, pulling towards a bend in the river.

As we neared the bend *THUMP-CRACK!* another shell hit a boulder, shooting fragments of rock like shrapnel across our canoes. I heard Park swear and grab his arm. Then we were around the corner and out of sight of the tank.

"Fast!" yelled Jock. "Keep moving!" He grabbed his radio and gave base our position.

"You know, this sort of thing would be a helluva lot easier with GPS," Park grunted as he tried to paddle with one arm.

And then the shells stopped and I heard the sound of an incoming helicopter. This was it—we were doomed! A spotlight shone down on us from above and I waited for the coming hail of bullets. Instead, I heard an amplified voice.

"We've got you covered—keep moving."

It was an Ulimbese gunship. Thank Ares.

It opened up on the enemy with rotating machine guns so fast they sounded more like tearing paper than individual shots.

You know, I almost felt bad for breaking a few of those airships.

Jock and I kept paddling until we saw lights ahead—our boys at last. We pulled up on the bank, handing over the prince and bundling him into the back of an armored transport. A scattered group of rebels in canoes came in behind us, some with injuries. A medic took Park aside and got a tourniquet on his arm, then started working on the Ulimbese, getting them stabilized and on the trucks.

As I sat in the dark, wet and chilled and overclocked from adrenaline I found myself wishing for just one thing. A hot shower. A hot shower with Aurora in it.

Okay, maybe that was two things. Putting business before pleasure really was a drag. I promised myself that when this was all over, I'd go back and pay Aurora a little visit.

That was when I remembered we'd blown up her place of employment, possibly with her in it. Damn.

Chapter 12

The Betrayal

Someone tossed me a blanket and the rest of the night disappeared. The next morning I woke up stiff and out of sorts in the back of a parked truck. Gotta catch Zs when you can, I suppose, but I surprise even myself sometimes.

Now that we had the prince in custody, I figured we probably had this gig in the bag. I couldn't have been more wrong.

I staggered out of the truck in search of coffee and something to eat only to discover life had gotten more interesting in the night.

"Tommy," said Park. "You're up. Something's wrong, man. They're out of here."

"Who?" I said, rubbing my eyes and looking at wispy clouds streaking across the early morning sky.

"Ulimbese," he said, waving his arm towards the former position of our allies. He was right. They were gone.

"What the hell?" I said. "Trouble back home?"

"Dunno," said Park, "but Colonel Emerson send two of the brass to run down the head honcho and find out what's cooking."

"Yeah?" I said, "how long ago was that?"

"Maybe a half-hour," Park said. "Ward saw them go. Scuttlebutt is that the colonel had no advance warning. They started leaving around midnight. Everyone thought it was some organizational shakeup or something. Now, who knows."

"I don't fancy being left in our under-supplied state deep inside enemy territory," I said. "But I need some coffee. Let's steal some from the command tent."

Park shook his head. "Coffee dampens my primary survival skill." He twitched his trigger finger at me. "I drink nothing but water and tiger blood."

"That's fine for you," I said, "but if I don't get some some coffee I'll die."

I got to the tent and hunted down the major, who snuck me a cup of the good stuff.

"Damnedest thing, them pulling out," he said. "We got nothing from them on radio, no runner, no advance warning. Nothing. I don't like it, though. And the colonel isn't exactly copacetic about it either."

My gut twisted inside me. If the colonel's radar was buzzing, then, we were likely in real trouble. This was rapidly going from bad to worse. Corwistal had no love for us, and if they managed to convince the Ulimbese to turn on us, or hell, even just to pull back and leave us without support inside Corwistalian territory, we could find ourselves in well over our heads here.

Then I heard the squeal of tires and two of the colonel's aides pulled up in their jeep, slamming it into park and jogging towards the command tent, faces pale. I heard their voices inside, plus what sounded like swearing, then the colonel himself stepped out, talking furiously into a trans-orbital com. Something serious was happening. Captain Marks and other brass assembled and we gave them space.

A few minutes later, Marks came and pulled Kilo Company together.

"Gentlemen," he said, "we have a situation. As some of you know, we were to have extracted a certain member of the royal family last night. A cousin of the king. He failed to show and we instead captured the crown prince." He paused and chewed his lip for a moment, then continued. "As you may or may not have realized already, our

Ulimbese allies have withdrawn, leaving us alone outside a large, hostile city in which there are plenty of enemy units. We are informed that this withdrawal is due to the cousin's capture and torture, from which event crucial information about our client's desire to install a new government was obtained. The King of Corwistal, who has now been fully apprised of the situation, has decided to break his contract with Gruppo ENIL-EX and made a deal with their rival."

"What the hell is this all about, Jock?" I whispered.

"Shut up and listen," he snapped back.

"Of course, the king's chief priority is to get his son and heir back. Now that he's cut a deal with our employer, the Ulimbese have decided there's nothing in it for them and they have conveniently placed the responsibility for the death of the previous crown prince on our shoulders."

"That's legit," I pointed out to Jock, who nodded.

"The upshot is that they are leaving us hanging as an apology of sorts to the Corwistalians and the royal house."

There was a chorus of angry murmurs but the captain waved us down. "Stow it for now. There's no time to cry about this. The colonel has called for an extraction ASAFP, but we cannot be safely embarked this deep inside Corwistalian territory. We're going to retreat in an orderly manner to somewhere our transport can land without being shot down, and we're getting out of here within the hour. We've got the prince as insurance, so that should buy us the time we need. Get ready to roll and I will have further orders for you shortly. Dismissed."

"Damn," Park said from behind me. "We should have nuked the city."

Jock shrugged as we headed back to load up. "Blowing stuff up isn't the answer to everything."

"Don't knock it 'til you try it," Park said. He was visibly angry. We all were.

I started loading up ammo and MREs into one of our few trucks, alongside Ward, Jones and a couple of guys from Bravo company.

"I heard about last night, Tommy," Ward said. "Nice work."

"Thanks," I said, "I knew those river trips as a kid would come in handy eventually."

"Yeah," said Ward, "but next time, I want a piece of the action."

"Yeah?" I said. "Wouldn't you be afraid we'd shoot some kids or something?"

Ward grunted as he swung a box of mortar rounds onto the truck. "You got me wrong, Tommy. I saw plenty of action in my previous career. I may be a private here, but I'm no POG. I won't run."

I shrugged. He may or may not have been right about his distaste for killing the crew on the freighter, but that wasn't our call. And we were all stuck now. Screw it. I stuck my hand out and he shook it.

"We're all in this together now," I said. "I think we're all about to get more than we bargained for, unless the colonel can pull a rabbit out of his ass."

"Or a prince," he said.

"Yeah, let's hope that slows them down. We'd better pray his royal daddy actually likes him."

"This is taking too long," Jones said. "We'd better pull out of here soon."

"Tommy, Ward, Jones, good," said Jock, jogging up to us. "Was looking for you. Captain Marks is asking for volunteers."

"There you go," I said to Ward, then I turned to Jock. "For what?"

"Captain wants a rear guard. Park is already with me. I want you men in it."

"You sure about that? First we lost Rocky, then Leighton and Four-eyes bought it at the supply drop. This is a clusterfrag of epic proportions so far. Can't you find somebody else?"

Jock shook his head. "Come on, Tommy. If we're going to get out of here, we need our best men keeping them off our tail. And we are the best."

I looked at Jones. He nodded. "I'm in," said Ward.

"Fine," I said as he waited with a raised eyebrow. "I'm in. I can't let you and Park get killed without being there to say 'I told you so.'"

"That's the spirit," Jock said. "Follow me."

We stood in a valley, lined up in neat rows, waiting for the Corwistalians to arrive. There were forty of us, all volunteers taken from different squads in Kilo. Our two transports were parked behind the captain's jeep, beside which stood the prince and Captain Marks in the middle. Sweat trickled down my neck even though the watery sun above wasn't doing much to warm the meadow. There was still frost in patches among the dead brown grass, even though the afternoon was fading away.

"This is insane," I whispered to Park. "We're giving up our free pass."

He shrugged. "The prince has arranged for our safe passage."

I snorted. "Yeah, like we did for his older brother, right? How did that work out for him?"

I could hear the sound of engines approaching and the clatter of tracks grinding up the ground, but didn't see anything yet. The seconds ticked by like hours, and we still stood and waited. This was supposed to go down at thirteen hundred and it was rapidly approaching.

The prince stood patiently beside Captain Marks about twenty meters in front of my position, clad in a military jumpsuit, but standing proudly erect as befit his royal status.

First five tanks crested the hill. Then I heard the sound of rotors and two gunships followed behind the tanks. The tanks spread out across our front and were followed by squad after squad of soldiers marching in formation. Behind them came six armored cars armed with .50 caliber machine guns, all six of which were aimed in our direction. Holy St. Possenti on a flaming cross! If they were going for intimidation, it was working.

We had our guns at the ready, plus four RPG teams and a machine gun mounted on the jeep, but if someone started shooting, there was no way we would get out. No chance at all. My blood felt like ice and like everyone else, my eyes went to the captain. He turned and nodded back to us, cool and collected, with a half-smile on his face. The catch in my throat eased slightly, but I knew we were taking a hell of a gamble. What was the captain thinking? Why not just keep the goddam prince until our transport arrived?

A second pair of gunships flew up from the city, then split up to take positions hovering over our left and right flanks. Fantastic.

I looked at Jock and saw his jaw working. He knew what we were up against. If the prince decided to betray us, this would be our grave. I remembered how we had manhandled the young royal out of the whorehouse, naked, helpless, and humiliated, and grimaced. He had no reason to love us.

We were surrounded now. I watched as machine gun teams set up on the hillside as two more armored transports crested the ridge and rapidly flanked us. We knew they wouldn't shoot yet, but what would happen when we gave up the prince?

Then a glossy black off-road vehicle pulled to the front of the enemy line, followed by four military jeeps. They stopped about fifty meters from our men and a Corwistalian general in an ostentatious blue parade uniform stepped out of the SUV as a dozen royal guardsmen in battle armor jumped out of the jeeps behind him.

They hung back just behind the general, letting him take the lead. He walked directly up to Captain Marks, inspected the prince, then spat on the ground in front of the captain. We clutched our rifles tighter. I was ready to shoot the arrogant prick there and so was every other Wardog there, but we knew it was a fight we could not win.

"I see your allies have withdrawn," the general sneered. "So, what are we to do with you soldiers of ill-fortune?"

"My understanding is that we will turn over the prince to you, then be allowed to safely depart," the captain said. He nodded to the prince, who did not deign to take notice before being escorted to the black SUV by a pair of the royal guardsmen.

"Now we have what we came for, mercenary," the General said scornfully. He raised his hand and the men behind them raised their weapons and aimed them at us. "Which leaves only the inconvenient matter of your murder of a prince of the royal house. Tell your men to lay down their arms, Captain, and they will be provided with a fair trial."

Sure we would. All our guys had responded by bringing up our own weapons and targeting a Corwistalian. The situation was hopeless, but we would take out as many of the little bitches out as we could before they sent us to Hell.

"Hold your fire, men," Captain Marks said evenly, then addressed the general. "General, we were promised safe passage upon the return of the prince. He is unharmed, as promised. So, let us depart in peace. If you attack us now, I promise you, you will all die with us."

"Die?" said the general with a dry laugh. "With what army do you intend to bring this to pass?"

Marks smiled grimly. "Do you see this jeep? Inside, on the floor on the passenger's side, is a tactical nuke shell that is rigged with a deadman's switch."

A look of confusion flashed across the general's face, but he recovered quickly and laughed. "You're bluffing."

The captain shrugged indifferently. "Go have a look for yourself."

The general stared at the captain as if trying to read his mind by sheer force of will. Whatever he saw in Marks's eyes convinced him not to take any chances.

"Commander, examine the jeep," he barked at one of the royal guards. The man nodded briskly and complied. He opened the side door, leaned over, and then recoiled as if he'd seen a winged Kolomese viper.

"Probably don't want to slam that door too hard, Commander," the captain commented. Some of the Wardogs laughed. Not me. I was too busy trying to control my bladder, not unlike the general, whose face had gone paler than pale.

What sort of ice-cold bastard rigs a nuke to blow and then practically holds it in his lap? My respect for the captain's stones grew ten sizes that day.

"V-v-very well," the general finally managed to say after swallowing hard two or three times. "The prince did grant you safe passage and it would be a stain on his honor were we to fail to respect his word."

"You are a true man of honor, General." How the captain managed to say that with a straight face, I'll never know.

The general waved at his men to stand down and nodded to the captain. He stood there at parade rest as if he didn't have a care in the world, but I saw the beads of sweat forming at his hairline.

I breathed a sigh of relief myself. The captain had done it, the crazy SOB! A little insurance on a smooth transfer. If things had gone south and the nuke was triggered, well, at least Wardogs would have had its revenge. Of course, that would have been small comfort to those of us caught in the blast zone.

"Load up, men," the captain ordered. "Let's get the hell out of here before they change their minds. On the double—go-go-go!"

We didn't hesitate to rush into the vehicles, knowing that at any moment the general could change his mind and blow us all straight to the Devil. Even without the tac-nuke in the jeep, there were so many barrels, tubes, missiles and hostile stares aimed our way that our weeping ladies back home would be lucky to get a fingernail to bury.

Our three vehicles raced down the hill and up the other ridge, tracked by the enemy guns the entire way. No sooner had we crossed the second ridge and descended the other side than there was a massive *KER-BOOM* that thumped you right in the depth of your chest, following by a tremendous shockwave that shook the ground all around us. It was as if there had been an earthquake. We all spun around to look back at the ridge, only to see a huge column of glowing smoke and fire rising up from the other side in the telltale shape of a mushroom.

As we watched, one of the gunships spiraled down into the ground. The other one had simply vanished from the sky.

"What?" I yelled to Jock over the whistling of the wind. "What in the hell just happened?"

To my surprise he was laughing. "He had two!"

"Two what?"

"Two nuke shells. Captain Marks must have had the second one buried in the hilltop before we got there!"

I whistled, astonished and more than little appalled by the captain's ruthlessness. How the hell did he get Colonel Emerson to sign off on a gamble like that? I knew the sub-sector execs back on Kantillon certainly hadn't.

The mushroom cloud in the sky behind us would have been easily visible from the city. We weren't pursued, and we were pretty damn sure that the entire enemy force had been obliterated. We had not only gotten clear, we'd whacked the general, the surviving crown prince, and about a company's worth of their royal guard. I started laughing, as the stress of the past hour melted into a giddy joy that bordered on insanity. We were all bastards, but Captain Marks was most definitely the stonest, coldest bastard of all. I felt a fierce and ferocious pride. Damn, but it felt good to be Wardog!

"Now *that* was off the chain," I told Jock.

"Damn straight!" He grinned happily. "Off the freaking chain!"

Chapter 13

The Retreat

We picked up a farm road through the woods and headed back towards the rest of the retreating Wardogs in high spirits. We weren't out of the sticks yet, but the general feeling was jubilant. We'd snatched a serious win from the jaws of defeat. Hell, we'd blown defeat's head right off!

Jock had the radio and we all heard Captain Marks give us the update on our plan. Jock was worried about fallout from the nuke but he told us it was some sort of clean nuke that wasn't radioactive like the older shells. Now we were to catch up with 2nd Battalion as soon as we could. We were guessing it would be about two hours before we caught up, since we could move a lot faster than they could. I kicked back with an MRE and wolfed it down, suddenly realizing I was starving. It was an Ulimbese-issue kit and the food tasted a little strange. The last thing I pulled out was some sort of candies in a roll. I unrolled the package and was about to try one when Park shook his head at me.

"Those are bad ju-ju. Throw them out."

"Seriously?" I said.

Jock shrugged. "Seriously. Locals say you eat those things and boom, your luck is shot."

"That's stupid," I said, popping a handful of the tart candies into my mouth. "Besides, I don't see how anything can go wrong now."

And then, without warning, our vehicle abruptly stopped. We looked at each other, puzzled. Then we heard the distant whop-whop-whop of rotors. Corwistalian gunships incoming.

"Now you done it," Park said, glaring at me as we snatched up our rifles. "Dammit, Tommy!"

"Forget your gun," Jock said to Park. "Grab the SAM launcher. I'm with you. Ward, you're with us too. Out into the open. Everyone else, run for cover."

The first gunship opened fire as we jumped from the transport. It was armored, but it wouldn't stand up long to the heavy machine guns with which the gunships were armed. I hit the ground hard, rolling upright, then made it into the trees as fire rained down from above.

"Spread out and shoot back," Captain Marks yelled at us as a gun-ship started a strafing run. Splinters of wood and clods of dirt flew all around me as I jammed in next to a tree and waited for an opening. There was a gap and I jumped to my feet, opening up with my rifle at the belly of the gunship as it swung overhead through the tree canopy.

Then I heard the *tick-CRACK-WHOOSH!* of the SAM firing from behind me, and saw the streak of smoke rip across the sky towards the banking gunship. I heard something explode above us, but from my angle I couldn't see if it was a hit.

"Missed him," Jones shouted. "Look north! North!"

I ran up to the edge of the treeline to see what was coming, only to see there were two more gunships hovering on the horizon.

"Dammit!" Jock shouted. "That was our only shot."

"They don't know that," Captain Marks yelled, coming up through the brush to my left. "Hang tight and stay down." He spoke into his com quickly, staring up at the squadron of gunships as they swung lazily through the air, keeping their noses towards our position, but refraining from coming any closer.

"They're locking missiles on the transports," I said, feeling my skin prickle with tension. We could probably get away from them thanks to the trees, but without our rides, the Corwistalians would run us down before we could join up with the regiment.

"Just stay cool," Marks reiterated firmly.

I was already down on the ground but I kept my eyes on the distant gunships. Then the first gunship fired; I could see the puffs of smoke under each wing, followed almost immediately by a pair of explosions barely forty meters in front of it. The second gunship fired a salvo, but its two missiles immediately began corkscrewing through the air, flying off in different directions before exploding harmlessly in the distance.

Malfunctions? Shoddy construction? Corrupt defense contractors? Or just bad ju-ju? There was no way that just happened! Four consecutive misfires?

The gunship pilots appeared to be considering a similar line of thought, as a thin trail of smoke began rising from the gunship that had fired first. The third gunship fired a burst from its guns that hit the ground nowhere near the three abandoned vehicles, then the whole squadron swung around in unison and beat a hasty retreat.

"Captain!" Jock shouted. "What the hell was that?"

Marks smiled at him and winked, as he buttoned one of the pockets on his torso armor. It was just big enough for a small device. A small technologically advanced device, about the size of a Norton Directed EMP Jammer.

"Did you do that, Captain?" Jock pressed Captain Marks as we watched the gunships retreat from view. "What happened? How did you do that?"

"That was illegal," Park muttered in awe. "Totally and utterly illegal."

"I'll chip in to pay the fine," Ward said. I was with him on that one.

"Load 'em up," Marks said, ignoring the badgering as he led us back to our unscathed vehicles. "Let's get back to our guys."

"Maybe they just had a bad lot of missiles," Ward said as we got into the back of our truck. "But that was awfully suspicious."

I grinned. I knew exactly what the Captain had done. He'd broken Ascendancy law, to be sure, and probably the terms of our contract too, but he'd done so in a manner that would be almost impossible for anyone to prove even if the gunships were equipped with cams. And, more importantly, he had saved our butts. While I couldn't speak for the Corwistalians, I sure as hell wasn't going to file a complaint with whatever Ascendancy agency was responsible for policing the planetary tech levels.

"Crazy SOB," Jock said, pressing past us and opening the SAM case as Park jumped in behind him and packed it up. "Nukes first, now this. I wonder what else he's got up his sleeve?"

Or in his pockets, I thought. But I didn't say anything.

"We're ten kilometers from the regiment, men," came Captain Marks's voice crackled over the radio. "It probably won't surprise you to learn that it is being pursued by Corwistalian forces. The problem is that an armored column is between us and them."

"Do we have enough fuel to drive around them," I asked Jock and he nodded.

RAT-TA-TAT-TAT! I wasn't the only one who jumped as a spray of fire rattled off the armored rear of our transport.

"Incoming!" yelled one of the guys on the back. "Troop transports— no, more than one. Got a few coming! Four...no five."

Our little column was driving on a logging road through the woods with little space to maneuver. We were bringing up the rear, so we couldn't speed up or evade.

"Drop an RPG team, sergeant!" the captain ordered. Clearly he was aware of our situation. "Don't let them close in on you!"

I heard the engine roar and fell back against Park as the driver stepped on the gas. Captain Marks must have told the other two drivers to speed up to give us more time to drop the ambush.

For a moment it seemed we were leaving them behind, until we had to slow down to take a corner. *RAT-TA-TAT-TAT!* Another spray of fire struck the dirt perhaps 20 meters behind us. The road was winding and they weren't close yet, but we had nowhere to run.

"Roger!" Jock yelled. "Park, Jones! Take the RPG and jump after the next corner! I'll tell the driver to slow down!"

About a minute later, we rounded a curve, the truck's brakes screeched, and Jock slapped Park on the shoulder. "Go go go!"

The tires sent up a flurry of dirt that obscured our view of them as the driver gunned the engine again. Jock nodded, satisfied, as we saw the two of them setting up right in the middle of the narrow road. I didn't envy the inhabitants of the lead vehicle. The Ulimbese RPGs were crude and lacked accuracy at range, but packed a big punch. "That'll buy us a little time."

The radio crackled again. "Scotsman, eye in the sky says we're approaching a long curve which will blind them for about 20 seconds. Once your caboose rounds that corner I want everyone but the driver to debark and take up positions along one side of the road under cover. Set a mine to take out the lead, then neutralize the other two when they stop."

"Roger," Jock said. "On your signal, over." He grabbed a hefty bandolier and slipped it over his shoulder, then grinned at me. "Always be prepared. You're with me."

I nodded. Then, from behind we heard the familiar whuuush of an RPG firing, followed by an explosion and the rattle of machine gun fire. A moment later, Jock's radio crackled. "We took out the first one," Park said. "That slowed them down. We'll work our way back to you through the woods. Good luck, over."

"Bravo zulu boys," Jock praised them. "Now scoot and leave the rest to us."

"Scotsman," said the Captain, "prepare to exit on my signal." There was a pause and we waited tensely as our vehicles rounded a long corner, then braked hard enough to start sliding horizontally on the dirt. "Go go go!" the Captain yelled and we exited the rear as fast as we could, hitting the ground and rolling like we were landing a drop, then scrambled for the trees.

The roadside was rocky and thick with dead frost-burned brush beneath towering pines. I hoped we could stay out of sight as the cover was lousy thanks to winter taking the leaves of the shrubbery bordering the road.

Jock was already placing the mine. He jammed the device's legs into the curve of the roadside, pointing down the road in the direction from which the enemy was coming. I wrapped wire around another sapling about a meter off the road to secure the cable, then threw the spool back to Jock. He plugged it in, then ran to join me at the position I'd selected behind a fallen tree. Meanwhile, our guys had taken up positions to our left, setting up the kill zone. These archaic mines threw a 60-degree cone of death in front of them when the charge blew. This one was more of an anti-personnel device but it was powerful enough that it would take out the driver, and most likely, his gunner too.

I handed the end of the wire to Jock, who carefully inserted it into a little socket in his carbine. As soon as he gave that thing a squeeze, an electrical pulse would fire off the explosive in the back of the mine and take out the lead vehicle.

We were just in time. The roar of our pursuer's engines grew louder, and soon the vehicles were in sight.

"One…" I counted, "two…three…we've got three transports approaching."

"Good. Park and Jones got one, so at most they've got a platoon trying to find them in the woods."

The transports were moving fast. Closer…closer…I could make out the face of the young gunner on the top of the first one, squinting against the rain.

"A little closer," Jock said, "just a little more…and…"

CRACK-KOOM! He blew the mine and then I was firing a grenade at the side of the first vehicle as heard the rattle of our boys opening up from their position up the road. There was a crash as the second truck slammed into the first, crushing two soldiers who had been trying to get out the back. The gunner of the second truck had been thrown half out of his turret and I picked him off before he could get back to his gun.

The third transport had disgorged six or seven Corwistalians and the gunner was working over the trees not far from where Ward was taking cover. Jock pointed to him and shouted "cover me," then rushed toward the burning first truck. I flicked the switch on my Katzer to full auto, but waited until Jock edged past the second truck to pop up and empty my magazine.

The Corwistalians reacted as I had hoped, by hitting the deck, which gave Jock time to step out, kneel down, and line up his shot. He fired a grenade, which hit the turret and blew the top half of the gunner into the air. Losing their last heavy weapon took the fight out of the rest of them, and they threw down their guns before putting their hands in the air.

As Ward and the others stepped out of the forest, their weapons trained on the surrendered soldiers, Jock reached into one of his pockets. For a second, I thought he was going to toss a grenade at them, so I was relieved when he produced a handful of zips. You always want to leave the enemy an option that doesn't involve fighting you to the death, unless he leaves you no other choice.

While we zipped them up, Jock got in touch with Captain Marks. "Scotsman to Kilo One, it's all over here. Scratch three more transports. We took some prisoners, but we can't take them with us."

"Good work, Scotsman," came Captain Marks's voice. "Leave them alive. Get up here as soon as the RPG team joins you, we need to move fast."

"Load up!" Jock yelled and our guys ran past him towards our transport, Jock counting as they came. Not even an injury on this one. Corwistal was fighting Wardogs, I thought, spitting on the ground before jumping into the truck. Even using crappy low tech we were better than these retro dirtsiders.

Park and Jones showed up sooner than we expected. Turned out the troops from the fifth transport didn't chase them, but had loaded up with casualties from the one they took out and skedaddled instead. After they embarked and we drove off to rejoin Captain Marks, I was feeling pretty good about our chances for the first time since the Ulimbese sold us out.

We made good time for about two hours, then we reached an open ridge and saw the regiment way down below. And they were in trouble.

There were two squadrons of Corwistalian gunships circled warily overhead, staying just out of range of our AA missiles. The bigger problem was the line of a heavy infantry force dug in to the south, a whole division by the look of it, blocking our escape route back into Ulimbese territory.

I heard Park curse as he pointed down to the north where a gorge entered the valley, and then I saw the Corwistalian armored column pouring in a few kilometers from behind the regiment.

They were surrounded. We were cut off.

And I didn't think Captain Marks had any surprises in his pockets that were capable of dealing with a situation like this.

Chapter 14

The Extraction

We were standing next to our transports. Captain Marks was looking down in silence at the unexpected situation down below. I watched his face, looking for some reassuring sign, some indication that he had a plan, but nothing came. He knew the colonel had been outmaneuvered and we were beaten. There was nothing we could do to save the regiment.

We didn't even have a 75 to fire our one tactical nuke shell.

"I guess we were the lucky ones this time," Park said quietly. "I can't see how they'll get out of this."

"We need to join them," Ward said fervently. "They're our guys. We can't just watch them die."

"We'll all be dead if we jump into that mess," Jones said.

Jock shook his head. "Nobody's going to die today. They're going to demand our surrender. Maybe they hang a few officers, then they ransom off the rest of us to corporate."

The captain listened silently as we talked back and forth, then finally held up his hand. "Gentlemen, it seems to me we have two options, neither of them good. First option is we make our way down the ridge to join the regiment, and share their fate, whatever that might be."

There were murmurs of approval and disagreement, some men shaking their heads, others nodding silently. "The second one is that we drive on and make our way alone to a safe extraction point.

There's no guarantee that we'll make it, and there is even a chance that we'll get caught and killed while the rest of the regiment is ransomed."

Silence reigned as we watched the ants move far below. Truth be told I was torn. I was in Wardogs for the money. We all were. We bragged about it. But still, when you fight alongside guys, they become like your brothers. You don't just leave your family to die or to be sent off to a prison camp. But on the other hand, our one platoon wouldn't make a lick of difference to a regiment caught between an anvil of infantry and a hammer of armor. What would we be dying for? Honor? We were mercs, not soldiers.

"You know," Jock said reflectively. "That King of Corwistal has got to be ten kinds of pissed at us. I can't say I'd blame him if he didn't give us any quarter."

"You saying we should steer clear and try to get out on our own?" Ward demanded.

"I'm just saying we shouldn't assume they'll let the colonel surrender the regiment. And anyway, we know they'll probably hang the captain. And I'm not down with that."

"I can't I'm enthusiastic about the concept myself, Sergeant," Captain Marks admitted. "But if we abandon them and somehow make it off-planet, we will have to live with that knowledge…and see it in the faces of every Wardog down there who survives."

"I say we roll the dice with our boys," I heard myself saying, almost as if someone else was speaking for me. It sure sounded a lot more stupid than anything I was normally likely to say.

"Me too," said Ward. Jones shook his head as if he was against the idea, but then he said, "Well, I guess you can count me in too."

One by one, every man in the platoon pledged to go down that hill. Jock was the last to declare himself.

"I figure you boys will need me to look after you in the camp. Tommy, you're too pretty and we don't want you ending up some toothless Ulimbese sergeant's prison bitch."

The others laughed. "So, you think they'll let us surrender, Sarge?" Park said hopefully.

"Nah, that's if we're lucky. They'll probably just clusterbomb us. Maybe a nuke, if the king is mad enough."

The captain cleared his throat. His face was somber, but his eyes sparkled with grim amusement. "If you're quite done encouraging the men, Sergeant, I suggest we start figuring out a way to get down there alive."

He looked around at the rest of us. "I'm proud of you men. Damned proud of you all."

Somehow, and I don't know why, that seemed to make it all worth it. We got back into the trucks, heads high, no fear, and all hesitation gone. I felt calmly certain that I was going to die, and I wasn't afraid either. I had no fear, only resolve. I would take as many of these dirtside toy soldiers with me as I possibly could, then die laughing on a pile of their corpses.

Dusk fell and gave us cover as we took a winding road down into the valley. We had to race like hell to be sure to get there ahead of the approaching armor, but somehow, we made it back to rest of the Wardogs without encountering the enemy. The colonel himself saw our trucks pulling in and walked over to greet Captain Marks.

"Welcome back," he said to the captain, loud enough for all of us to hear. "All of you need to know what we face. We're in deep. This morning our scouts made contact with enemy infantry ahead, waiting for our arrival. They're dug in, with cannon pointed our way, machine guns, howitzers, you name it. Then to either side we have the mountains reaching upwards. From behind, we have a large column of armor. And here we are in the middle, our last drone down, lacking supplies, low on ammo and pinned. We have enough antiaircraft missiles left to keep the gunships from getting too close, but they've got all the time in the world. Right now they're just bringing in the armor behind us, then I fully expect they'll bomb us to hell."

The captain nodded. "Have they offered any terms, sir?"

"Way-ull," the colonel drew it out. "They sent me a little note. Said they'd let us all go for the price of half our contract, so long as we turned over the officers responsible for the deaths of both princes."

The two officers shared a long look. "Officer," Captain Marks said. "There was only one officer responsible."

Next to me, Jock took a sharp breath. We all knew the captain wouldn't hesitate to trade himself for Kilo company, let alone the entire regiment.

"What did you tell him?" Captain Marks asked calmly, as if his life was not on the line."

Colonel Emerson grinned. "What do you think I told him, Captain? I told him that he'd better tell his men to get the hell out of our way or we would kill every man jack of them!"

The men roared. An impromptu cheer went up. "Wardogs, Wardogs!" I swear, at that moment, we would have stormed the gates of Hell itself if the colonel had ordered it.

Despite his unasked-for reprieve, the captain's face hadn't changed expression. "So what's the plan?"

The colonel nodded in approval. "We need to hit their infantry and break through before that armor can lay into us from behind. They are dug in and we'll be advancing right into the teeth of those machine guns. But that's our only play."

The captain nodded. "We're good to go. Where do you want us?"

"Join Major Skelton and the rest of the 2nd on the right flank," the colonel said. "We start the assault at nightfall, so twenty hundred ten. God be with you, men."

We returned his salute and made our way to where the rest of Kilo company was positioned on the east.

I looked around at our guys, spread across the field. We were almost all on foot, with transports for maybe one-fourth the men, supported by ten howitzers and maybe twenty mortars. We did not have a single tank. I cursed the Corwistalians, I cursed the weaselly Ulimbese, and above all, I cursed the bastards at whatever cheap-ass shipping company had left us here without our armor. For good measure I cursed whatever paper-pusher at corporate had hired that company. And while I cursed them all, I cleaned my Katzer carefully, polishing and re-polishing every part as the clock ticked slowly closer to go.

"Tommy," said Jock.

"Yeah?" I said, leaving my reverie. "What?"

"Good work. On this mission. We did everything right."

I snorted. "Maybe. But that won't save our asses this time."

"We'll see," Jock said, winking as if he knew something I didn't, but I knew he was just trying to keep my spirits up. "Keep the faith, Tommy. Always keep the faith."

The order to advance was given, then our artillery opened up, focusing on a small area of the enemy line through which we were hoping to break. We were rushing through the darkness towards the enemy infantry. They were perhaps a half-kilometer ahead of us and I saw their guns open up on our charge as we advanced into the arms of death. I could see the enemy in my thermals, guns blazing like white-hot suns, the cooler heat signatures of infantrymen aiming at us, and us running like moths towards the flame, as our big guns boomed behind us.

Then six starshells were launched high above the battlefield and the Corwistalian artillery began to fire. They had sighted in their guns before darkness fell and we had entered the killing zone. I didn't even hear the shell that exploded nearby, but felt myself leave the ground completely as a shockwave hurled me sideways into the mud.

Then another struck nearby, and another. I screamed and tried to keep crawling forward, but I was too stunned and scared to push myself back to my feet. Another Wardog pulled me to my feet, just in time for another shell to come in, this time in front of us, that blinded me for a moment as my goggles went instantly dark to preserve my eyesight.

"Keep moving forward!" he yelled at me, pulling my arm. "We can't stay here!"

Another shell burst, then another, and then a strange bolt of green fire lit up the mountainside forward and to our left, catching our attention despite the deadly hellfire exploding all around us. I heard a cheer go up from hundreds of throats and then another flash of green hellfire stabbed down at the mountain again, and again, and again. We stared at the sight in awe…and realized that there were suddenly no more shells incoming.

"Holy deep space!" the Wardog shouted, echoing my own thought. "That was from freaking *orbit*! They came for us! They came!"

Gradually, the rattle of machine gun fire from the enemy ahead trailed off, as did the returning fire from our men. "Cease fire, cease fire!" came the order, passed man-by-man through the ranks. "Cease fire!"

Jock and Park found us a few moments later "I told you!" Jock said triumphantly, slapping me on the back. "Didn't I tell you to keep the faith! The ship targeted their artillery from orbit and the Corwistalians contacted the colonel right away. We've got passage through, they're letting us through!"

"Good call," I laughed. "They don't want us blasting their entire military from space."

"But how did they do it?" said Park. "As much as I am now a fan of orbital strikes, they're not exactly legal."

"The hell with that, we know how they did it," Jock said. "They put those dirtside guns in the crosshairs and hit the red button. Everybody has a price, and whatever it cost to pay someone to look the other way, that was cheaper than replacing us."

I wasn't sure what he meant until I saw Park rubbing his fingers together. Ah, yes. That made sense. Wardogs Inc. must have paid off someone in the Ascendancy's planetary tech police office—hell, maybe we paid off the whole damn office—in order to save the regiment.

I silently retracted all the horrible things I'd said about our paper-pushers. Clearly Wardogs not only had the best mercs in the industry, we had the best white-collar men too.

An hour later we walked through the lines of the Corwistalian infantry, brightly lit by their portable lights. They grumbled and spat and cursed at us as we passed, but we didn't care. They were getting out of our way, just like the colonel told them to. No one made any move to stop us.

I looked to my left at Park, Jones and Ward. Then to my right at Jock and Marks. Rocky, Four-eyes and Leighton should have been with us, by rights, but they were with us in spirit even though their bodies would remain here, on this strange planet. We walked through the enemy, our heads high, even as the royal soldiers looked at us with unbridled hatred in their eyes. We'd come to their planet, killed members of the royal family, helped their hated enemies steal their land, nuked their soldiers on their territory, and here we were getting off-planet almost scot-free. I didn't blame them for hating us, but they really shouldn't have. We were just doing our jobs. And if we did a damn good job of it, well, we were professionals and that's just what professionals do.

Walking through the gauntlet of jeers and hatred made me feel closer to my fellow Wardogs. I felt no shame or even anger at the hissing and cussing directed our way. Instead, I felt a deep pride. We'd overcome the odds, we'd overcome the local treachery, our brass had stood by us and got us through in the end. We'd go on to fight again, cashing in again on world after world, planet after planet, while these dirtsiders would serve their petty king on their agro-planet, fighting over farmland with each other until they finally retired to their dumpy wives and crummy farms.

They were just cogs in a crude machine. But we were Wardogs, the best and the most profitable of the best.

By the time we made it over the border it was nearing midnight. We had been so close to safety, but they had the numbers and their position had been strong and deep. Without the intervention of our men in orbit, there's no way we could have broken through them.

The wispy clouds above lit up ahead as our transport descended. Above it I saw its fighter escort, two wickedly slender atmo-capable craft, circling on high like bats in the sky, silent and lethal. They were a powerful message to any king or emperor who might try to get cute and fire a missile as we were exiting the planet. They were a reassuring sight indeed.

It was dawn before we finally finished loading and embarked. I ended up strapped in between Ace and Jock.

"Hey Tommy," Ace said.

"Hey, Ace! What have you been up to?"

He laughed. "Not much. Got shot, and thanks to the caveman-level med-tech here, I nearly lost my damn leg." He indicated his right leg, which was bound up in a black compression bandage. "Is it just me or did this contract kind of suck?"

"Yeah, tell me about it," I said. "One screwup just led to another. Almost made me think I was back in the army."

"No," said Jock, "if this had been the army, we'd all be prisoners right now. Or dead. Twice over."

He was right. But still...I looked around. Everyone looked beat. Faces bleeding, bruised, unshaven, battle armor caked with mud, exhausted.

There was a chime and the transport pilot's voice came over the intercom. "Wardogs, we will be leaving the planet shortly. Please be sure your butts are properly strapped in as said butts will soon be hurtling into space at a rate of speed far beyond the normal velocity of butts. Thank you for flying with Wardogs Space Lines and we hope you enjoy your flight."

The engines roared and I felt my bones vibrate, then I was pressed heavily back into my seat as we rocketed up towards the safety of orbit, leaving this miserable world behind. The thrill of being rescued had now subsided and we were all feeling seriously beat. Once the acceleration evened out, a regular bitchfest began concerning everything from the Ulimbese throwing us under the bus to the stupid shipping company to the fact that corporate had somehow managed to let us go through all that madness without ever being able to get us properly equipped.

I felt weary down to the center of my bones. Yeah, we'd survived, but barely. I was seriously considering turning in my resignation after this one. It could easily have been Four-eyes up here and me down there dead. Luck had carried me through this time, but every man on board here knew that Lady Luck was a fickle bitch who let you down when you least expected it.

"Wardogs," the colonel's voice came over the intercom, "this is Colonel Emerson. We are nearing the KCS *Ridgeback* and you now have access to the ship's intranet. If you have access, I suggest you may want to log in to your personal accounts at this time. Thank you for your dedication, your discipline, and your hard work. That is all."

Jock fumbled in his pack and pulled out his comm, then ran his fingers over it for a moment. I saw his mouth open, then close. He blinked, frowned, then wordlessly handed me the device.

"What?"

"Just log in," he told me.

I did as he suggested, wondering what had surprised him. And then my account popped up. I wasn't rich, not yet, anyway. But I was a damned sight closer to rich than I'd been a month ago.

"Not bad," I said with a smile, staring at those big beautiful numbers on the screen, all thoughts of retirement leaving my mind in a heartbeat. "Now that's not bad at all!"

THE END

The WARDOGS INC. series continues with Book 2:

Hunter-Killer

CPSIA information can be obtained
at www.ICGtesting.com
Printed in the USA
FSHW012105070320
67891FS

9 789527 065082